THE ENCORE

C. Marie

*For anyone who has shrunk themselves to keep the peace.
For anyone who learned to survive before they learned to live.
Choose yourself anyway.
And may love always meet you there
—without asking you to be less.*

CONTENTS

Title Page

Dedication

PLAYLIST

Triggers

Chapter 1	1
Chapter 2	11
Chapter 3	25
Chapter 4	35
Chapter 5	51
Chapter 6	63
Chapter 7	77
Chapter 8	87
Chapter 9	99
Chapter 10	115
Chapter 11	131
Chapter 12	141
Chapter 13	153
Chapter 14	165
Chapter 15	177
Chapter 16	189

Chapter17	201
Chapter18	215
Chapter19	225
Chapter20	234
Chapter21	248
Chapter22	262
Chapter23	274
Chapter24	284
Chapter25	296
Chapter26	308
About The Author	319
Books By This Author	321

PLAYLIST

BARRACUDA - HEART
SHUT UP AND DANCE - WALK THE MOON
HOTEL ROOM SERVICE - PIT BULL
EVERLONG - FOO FIGHTERS
TIPSY - J-KWON
PLEASE EXCUSE THE MESS - ELLA LANGLEY
ALL MY EX'S LIVE IN TEXAS - GEORGE STRAIT
BROKEN - SEETHER & AMY LEE
ONLY WHEN IT'S YOU - BLEEDING VERSE
IT'S BEEN A WHILE - STAIND
WHEN YOU SAY NOTHING AT ALL - ALISON KRAUSS
NIGHTMARE - HALSEY

TRIGGERS

STALKING
PAST CHILDHOOD SEXUAL
ABUSE (NON-GRAPHIC)
TRAUMA RECOVERY
PARENTAL ABANDONMENT/ABSENT PARENT
MANIPULATION
MILD LANGUAGE
MATURE THEMES
SEXUALLY EXPLICIT SCENES

THIS BOOK CONTAINS STALKING, REFERENCES
TO PAST SEXUAL ABUSE, EMOTIONAL
TRAUMA, AND CONFRONTATION WITH
AN ABUSER. THEMES OF HEALING,
EMPOWERMENT, AND PERSONAL RECOVERY
ARE CENTRAL TO THIS STORY.

Prologue
Lenni

The first man to teach me I couldn't rely on men was my father.

He didn't leave with a slammed door or a grand goodbye. No angry speeches. No final words.

He just... faded.

One day he was there—his boots by the door, his coffee cup on the counter—and the next he wasn't, as if someone hit mute on a whole person.

I was too young to understand it.

Old enough to learn people disappear anyway.

And if you're not careful, they take pieces of you when they leave.

So I clung to what stayed. I held my mama, because she never disappeared, and I held our sagging trailer together. It sat behind Miller's Salvage, half-hidden by pines and junked-out trucks, balanced on cinder blocks like it might give up if you leaned too hard.

Slateford wasn't a town that welcomed you—it tolerated you. Church on Sundays. Gossip by Monday. And if you came from where we came from, you learned quick to keep your head down and your mouth shut.

I watched Jolene Vale try to fill Dad's absence with men who smiled too easily. Men who promised her the world – and watched me instead of her.

My mama stayed soft where life tried to harden her.

Soft didn't mean safe.

Soft didn't mean protective.

She'd laugh a little too brightly, smooth her blouse, pretend she didn't hear what I heard. If I stiffened, if I tried to handle it, she'd murmur, "Don't be ugly, baby," or "Just stay close to me," like closeness could undo a man's intentions.

She loves me—fiercely, faithfully—but love isn't the same as guarding. And when she couldn't be the wall, I became it. I learned the locks. I learned the exits.

I learned how to read a room before anyone else noticed the danger in it.

Now I'm standing in a Nashville rehearsal warehouse with my name stenciled on a road case.

"Beyond my wildest dreams" sounds good on camera.

Seeing it stamped next to your set times feels like standing at the edge of something sharp.

Like a cliff.

Because climbing this high means there's farther to fall.

"Lenni," my mama whispers beside me, and

the way she says my name is the only thing anchoring me. "Baby... are you seeing this?"

Jolene is wearing her best jeans and a blouse she ironed twice. Her brown curls are perfect, like she's headed to church. She looks tiny here—dwarfed by lighting rigs, sound towers, and the men hauling gear.

But the only thing small about Jolene Vale is her stature. She's the reason I left that trailer with my ribs intact and my hope still breathing. Not because she fought for me. Because she loved me. Because she never stopped encouraging me.

I sling an arm around her shoulders. "I'm seeing it."

Her eyes glisten. "I can't believe this is real."

"Me neither," I say, trying to sound nonchalant. My voice does that thing it always does when I'm about to feel too much—turns flat, like a closed door.

Across the warehouse, Rowan is tuning our Strat's, Kaira taps a steady heartbeat on the drums, and Sienna leans against a case, arms crossed, radiating a silent warning that makes anyone think twice before messing with her.

My people. My sound. My backbone.

The kind of women who don't just love you—they stand behind you.

Mila Santos – my manager – cuts through the chaos like a scalpel, tablet in hand, dark hair slicked back, blazer sharp.

"Lenni," she calls without looking up. "Five minutes to run intro. Jolene, stay behind the barrier during cues. No wandering."

Mama nods. "Yes, ma'am." Immediate. Automatic. Like permission is the only way she knows how to exist in a room full of authority.

Mila finally glances up and locks eyes with me. "Eyes up."

I deliver what the world paid for—the smirk, the steel, the Lenni Vale that doesn't flinch. "Born ready," I say.

Ro's lazy, sharp voice carries over:

"She's fine. She's just doing that thing in the mirror again."

I flip her off with love.

Mama laughs softly, still surprised that I have friends who feel like family – people who don't leave, people who don't take. People who would've made half the men in Slateford cross the street.

I step into my mark, and the moment the intro track hits, everything shifts.

Then I become her.

Lenni Vale.

Leather and bite, and bruised honesty.

The girl who doesn't flinch, who turns pain into choruses and dresses it up like power. The girl who learned young that nobody was coming to save her—so she'd better look like she didn't need saving.

Even if some part of me still wonders what it

would feel like if someone did.

My voice locks in. Ro's guitar snarls. Kai's drums thunder. Sin's bass rolls through the floor.

It's flawless.

When we cut, my mama claps like she's at a stadium, hand over her mouth like she's trying to keep her feelings from spilling everywhere.

"That was—Lenni, that was *insane*," she breathes.

I grin. "You're biased."

"Damn right I am," she says, then cups my face and kisses my forehead the way she used to when I was little and scared. "I'm proud of you."

Pride was a luxury we rarely afforded growing up. We had survival. We had grit. We had making it work.

So when she says it, I nod like it doesn't rearrange my bones. Like it doesn't make something tender and angry rise in my throat at the same time.

Mila reappears, already moving the day forward. "Break for fifteen."

We head toward my dressing room area—a converted office with my name taped on the door.

My assistant, Harper James, hustles by with my water. Tessa Larkin trails her with my garment bag, all black eyeliner and sharp edges.

I open the door—and stop.

The room smells wrong. Too sweet. Too heavy.

On the vanity sits a bouquet. An eerie arrangement of white lilies, black roses, eucalyptus, and burgundy dahlias – beautiful in a way that feels intentional.

No card. No delivery slip. No florist label.

My pulse spikes, my vision narrows. I don't touch them. I don't move closer.

My pulse spikes. Vision narrowing.

Exits. Distance. Faces.

Every muscle shifts into the version of me that survived before anyone noticed danger existed.

"Mila," I call, my voice steady.

She's there in an instant, eyes scanning, hand already at her earpiece. "Nobody accepted any deliveries," she says, calmly. "Don't touch anything."

My mama's voice wavers behind me. "Lenni? Honey, what is that?"

I turn with a smile so smooth it scares me sometimes. "Just a fan thing. You know how people can get."

Mama grabs at that explanation like it's a life raft. She always wants the world to be kinder than it is.

But Mila's already moving, already closing the distance, already becoming the wall.

She leans in over the bouquet without touching it, scanning the stems, the paper, the placement.

Then her gaze catches on something tucked deep between the lilies: a folded scrap of notebook paper, torn edge, handwriting looping along the page.

She taps at it with her pen, slides it free, unfolds it. Her face doesn't change – and that's when my stomach drops.

She holds it low, out of my mama's sight. I read it anyway:

You still sing like fire.

Cold crawls up my spine.

Mila's voice is soft in my ear. "We're leaving. Now."

For a second, I'm not our tour. I'm in a trailer with a lock that never held."

And the first thought that hits—sharp as a blade—isn't about me. It's about Mama.
Because I can go anywhere and take my danger with me.

But she can't. She'd stay. She'd smile. She'd hope it passes.

And nobody is going to take care of Jolene Vale if I don't.

After rehearsal, I pull into a small complex tucked behind a line of trees—nothing flashy. Just clean, bright, secure. The kind of place with working locks and parking lot lights that don't burn out.

Mama stares at the building like it's a trick. "Where are we?"

I cut the engine. "Your new place. Happy Mother's Day."

Her face turns toward me, confusion cracking into fear. "Lenni, I can't—"

"You can." I unbuckle and look at her. "You're not staying in that trailer. Not anymore."

Her eyes fill instantly, soft as always. "Honey… I don't want you spending your money on me."

"I'm not spending it on you," I say too fast, too sharp—then soften. "I'm spending it on peace. On being able to leave for tour without waking up at three a.m. wondering if you locked a door that doesn't lock."

She presses her fingers to her mouth like she's trying to hold herself together.

"Lenni…"

"I don't want to move," she whispers, and it's the most backbone I've heard from her in years. "My life. My job. My routine."

Her eyes shine like she's pleading for permission to keep everything the same. "I don't want new, baby. I just… want my same."

Something sharp rises in me—grief and fury braided together. Because "same" almost swallowed us whole.

"I've been taking care of us since I was a kid," I say, and it tastes like metal. "Let me do it now when I actually can."

Mama shakes her head, small and stubborn. "I can keep working. I can find a job. I can—"

"Yes, keep working if you want," I cut in, voice firm enough to hold the line for both of us. "I'm not taking your life away."

I point at the building like it's evidence. "I'm just giving you a roof that holds." My throat tightens. "I want you under this roof, Mama. I want you safe."

Her shoulders sag—not quite relief, not quite surrender. Just the weight finally shifting off her spine.

I hand her a ring of keys. They jingle softly, loud in the car like a promise.

"Utilities are set," I add. "Your name."
"And I met your neighbor—Ms. Carver across the hall. She's nosy in the good way. She'll like you."

Mama blinks through tears. "You... met my neighbor?"

"I did a walkthrough," I say, deadpan.

She lets out a watery laugh. "Of course you did."

Inside, the apartment smells like new paint and clean linen. Sunlight pours in through the blinds. There's a small kitchen and a little couch. The quilt I picked out for the bedroom reminded me of her—floral and gentle and stubbornly bright.

Mama turns in a slow circle, hand over her chest. "Oh, Lenni," she whispers like a prayer.

I stand in the doorway, arms folded tight so I

don't shake. "You're safe here."

She really looks at me then, and I see it all at once: gratitude, guilt, and the quiet truth that she never knew how to be the shield.

"I'm sorry," she whispers.

My throat tightens. I don't let it show.

"I know," I say, because it's the only way I can hold us both without breaking.

Then, quieter: "Just… stay. Let me leave knowing you're taken care of."

Mama crosses the room and wraps her arms around me—soft and trembling, like love is the only weapon she ever had.

I hug her back, because she'll always be my home.

And when I step onto that tour bus and let the world watch Lenni Vale burn bright, I'll do it with one less fear clawing at my spine.

Because if nobody else stands between danger and the people I love – I will.

CHAPTER 1

Lennon

Tennessee

Of course I've played Tennessee plenty of times – it's home turf.

But tonight feels different. This isn't a sun-baked festival where smudged eyeliner goes unnoticed.

Tonight, my name towers over the lineup.

Tonight, I'm the reason people drove three hours, paid for parking, queued for merch.

The venue hums like a neon hive, and somewhere inside that buzz—among the heat and roar and crackling anticipation—my body wants to betray me. But I won't let it.

That's Lenni Vale: knees knocking beneath a swagger that could part the Red Sea.

Control is the only thing nobody ever managed to take from me. Not men, not fear, not the past. Control means nobody sees the cracks unless I choose to show them.

Harper hovers at my dressing room door, clipboard in hand, practically vibrating with excitement. "The crowd tonight is off that charts – I mean absolutely wild. Merchandise is flying – "

"Harper," I interrupt, yanking my boot laces tight enough to cut off circulation.

She freezes. "Sorry. I'm just… this is your first headliner show."

I study my reflection. Armor: precise winged liner, smoky shadow, dark lips daring anyone to say something wrong. Hair piled into a messy half-up ponytail, long waves spilling down, effortless danger. Hoops in my ears, a nose ring glinting when I turn. Layered chains drape over a studded leather top. A fringe jacket hangs off my shoulders. Scuffed denim cutoffs look like I've lived in them.

The persona curated so carefully people forget there's a person under it.

Sometimes I forget too.

"Yeah," I say. "I noticed."

Harper's mouth twitches. "You're doing that thing."

"What thing."

"That thing where you pretend you're not nervous."

I lock eyes with myself. "I'm not nervous."

She gives me the look of someone who loves me and doesn't believe me. "Sure."

Two firm knocks—business. Mila slips in. "Opener's on. Thirty-minute move."

My stomach sinks. Opener. I've opened before. I've supported. I've played to chatting crowds. But tonight? Tonight a whole band warms them up for me.

Mila studies me. "You holding up okay?"

I tilt my head back. "Never better."

One sharp nod from her – she doesn't need to believe it. "Time to move."

The backstage corridor pulses with movement: crew hustling, cases rolling, radios crackling. I can feel the crowd's roar through the walls, like the venue itself has a heartbeat.

My gaze automatically tracks exits, security positions, blind corners. Habit. Instinct. Survival wrapped in muscle memory.

Hollow Mesa's guitars cut through the air—a raw, swaggering sound that's all whiskey-soaked Texas pride. Ro stands at stage left, arms crossed over her chest, black hair catching the lights. That knowing smirk of hers saying everything.

"They sound good," she says.

"They'd better," I mutter under my breath.

Ro chuckles, low and feral. "Honey," she says, nudging my shoulder with hers, not looking at me because she already knows where my head is. "remember whose crowd this is. Remember who you are. They're just stoking the fire for you now."

Something pounds beneath my ribs.

Ro has been with me since the beginning of time — since dive bars with broken monitors and motel rooms that smelled like cigarettes.

My crowd. My chaos translator. The one who turns my nerves into gasoline instead of fear.

Sin slides into view next, bass hanging from her shoulder, copper hair pulled back tight. Her eyes find mine, steady and unreadable.

Sin doesn't waste words – she anchors instead.

"Take a breath, Lenni," she says quietly.

Not a suggestion.

A calibration.

We picked her up at a show years ago when she first landed in Nashville — half-pissed at the world, half-exhausted, carrying more silence than sound — and she never really left.

I release air I didn't realize I was holding.

Kai appears behind her, drumsticks already tapping a restless rhythm against her thigh, blonde ponytail swinging like momentum incarnate.

Bam Bam, they used to call her in foster care – because shew as always hitting something, always making noise so she wouldn't disappear.

She gives us a quick chin lift – not a smile, not softness – just acknowledgement.

Colby's band wraps up their final song, and the arena transforms into a living thing—thousands of arms reaching skyward, fingers splayed. The crowd's voice becomes one thunderous pulse: "LEN-NI! LEN-NI! LEN-NI!"—drowning out the songs that play between sets.

My throat tightens. This can't be real.

For one dangerous second, I want to believe they're calling for *me* — not the version of me that never breaks, never hesitates, never needs.

But that version is easier to love.

So I give them her instead.

The stage manager's headset brushes my

shoulder as she leans close. "Time to shine, superstar."

I nod, smile dangerous. He cues me.

The intro track growls. Lights drop. One breath. One step.

I walk.

The curtain lifts. The crowd crashes over me. This room's bigger than my early gigs – mid-size but packed tight, build for sound and sweat and screams.

The barricade gleams, a thin line between me and hundreds of reaching hands.

I claim the spotlight before it claims me. Nerves be damned. I bring the mic to my lips.

" Tennessee," I drawl, letting the vowels stretch like taffy, the way Mama taught me to speak proper. "Y'all ready to burn this place down tonight?"

The crowd answers with a roar that vibrates through my bones. Ro strikes her first chord, Kai's drumbeat kicks in my chest, and Sin's bass line crawls up my spine.

When I open my mouth, that familiar smoke pours out – smoky alto with a raspy vibe – Miranda bite, Alanis confession, Stevie Nicks ache.

Country rock with bruises.

I sing grit, revenge, loving like war. They sing back like they've known me forever.

Halfway through the third song, I see the barricade flex.

Stage right—pressure ripples through the

front row like a tide. Bodies surge. Metal groans. Security shifts, shoulders tightening, heads turning in sync.

Normal – security everywhere.

Fine. I keep singing. Keep smiling. Keep being Lenni Vale.

Then my in-ear crackles: "Side corridor breach. Repeat: side corridor breach."

My breath stutters for half a second. Fingers tighten around the mic hard enough to ache.

I swallow it down and keep singing.

They don't get to watch me flinch. Not on my stage. Not in my song.

I hit the chorus harder, arm stretched skyward, eyes lit with that manufactured fire I've perfected—because if I look fearless long enough, the room believes it.

Ro catches my eye from the drums. Kai's fingers tighten on his guitar. Sienna widens her stance at the bass. My girls. My spine.

The music thunders on. So do I. We hammer through the bridge and crash into the finale. I take my bow like nothing touched me, like nothing ever does.

The second I'm behind the curtain, my knees threaten mutiny. Not because I'm weak – because adrenaline is a liar and it always collects its debt in the dark.

Mila appears, face grim. "Back room. Now."

I follow her, boots clicking sharp and steady, because that's what I do—move like I'm in charge even when my pulse is trying to climb out of my throat. The crowd's roar fades behind us, and the hallway swallows the light.

My fingers start to shake anyway.

Harper extends a water bottle. " Lenni—"

"I'm fine," I snap, and immediately hate the way it lands. Harper isn't the enemy. Panic is.

Mila's voice is clipped. "They got into the side corridor. Not fully backstage, but too close. They were intercepted."

"Who?" My throat tightens. "How did someone get in there?"

"Reviewing footage." Mila says.

I stare at the floor, forcing my hands to stop trembling through pure, stubborn will.

This should be my moment—local opener turned headliner, Tennessee screaming my lyrics.

Instead, I'm reminded that fame has seams, and some people spend their lives looking for where they split.

Evie Caldwell sweeps in, immaculate and commanding. Blonde hair sleek, perfect manicure tapping her iPad.

"Minimal statements." she says immediately. "No 'stalker' language. Call it a minor disruption, handled."

I lift my eyes. " I don' t want to discuss it at all."

Evie's gaze locks onto mine. "We're not talking about it. We're controlling it."

Mila folds her arms. "We're increasing protection."

My chest tightens.

"I don't need more guards," I say, the edge in my voice enough to draw blood. "I've handled myself this long."

Mila's doesn't blink. "And now you don't have to."

That's the problem.

Accepting protection feels like admitting I can't do it alone. Like I failed. Like I'm suddenly breakable.

I've spent my whole life being the one who watches the door. The one who notices the threat. The one who stands between trouble and the people I love.

I'm not built to be escorted.

Evie's tone stays cool. "New personal security detail starts tomorrow."

My stomach twists. Personal detail means someone shadowing every move, invading every space.

A babysitter with a badge and a superiority complex.

I straighten anyway, chin lifting, performer's mask sliding back into place like muscle memory.

"Fine," I say, voice smooth as polished stone. "Bring them in."

Evie nods like the situation belongs to her now—crisis managed, narrative shaped.

Mila's expression stays hard, like she's already

bracing for the next breach. I drop into a chair and listen to my name echo through the walls, the crowd still chanting like nothing can touch me.

I tell myself they haven't stolen tonight.

I tell myself the dream is still mine.

And I tell myself—harder than I believe it—that whoever they assign to "protect" me better understand one thing:

I'm not a doll.

I'm not a problem to solve.

And I don't need a damn babysitter.

CHAPTER 2

Harlan

Kentucky

By the time my plane lands in Kentucky and I get a ride, the venue is still asleep. I arrive hours before showtime anyway and park where I can watch both the main entrance and the loading dock without shifting my shoulders.

The building is quiet. Quiet doesn't calm me. Quiet makes me listen harder.

I collect my credentials, test the radios, eyeball camera placements. Then I walk the perimeter, checking every door, hinge, exit—each one filed away in my head. You see possibilities—and you close the ones that matter.

A sharp click of heels on concrete snaps me out of my thoughts. Mila Santos, tour manager, strides toward me – black hair pulled tight, tablet in hand, comms clipped to her collar. She sizes me up in one clean sweep like she's deciding whether I'll be useful or not.

"Harlan Godfrey," she says, like it's an item on her list.

"Yes, ma'am," I answer, my tone steady.

She doesn't relax. "You're early."

"I'm right on time."

A flicker—something close to approval—

crosses her eyes before she turns on her heel. "Come on."

I fall into step beside her, matching pace without crowding. People like Mila don't respect noise. They respect consistency.

She talks as we move, words clipped and efficient.

"Principal is Lennon 'Lenni' Vale. Inner circle is tight: PR is Evie Caldwell, stylist Tessa Larkin, assistant Harper James. You will not freelance press. You will not speak to fans. You will not step into camera frames unless necessary." Her gaze cuts to me, hard. "And you will not let her convince you she doesn't need you."

That tells me more about her than the file did.

"Understood," I say, the promise firm in my chest.

We reach a door labeled **LENNI VALE — DRESSING ROOM**.

Mila knocks twice, then swings it open without waiting for an answer.

"Lenni," she calls. "Your new security is here."

I step inside and immediately notice how tiny the room is for someone who owns every stage she walks on. But presence isn't measured in square feet.

Lennon Vale stands at the mirror, tightening a studded leather belt over faded denim. Each motion is so precise it looks choreographed.

Up close, she's even smaller than the stage makes her look, but there's nothing small about her presence. Compact muscle. Sharp lines. A stillness that says she's learned how to take up space without asking permission.

Like someone who learned early that space isn't given. Its defended.

Her hair is pulled back, messy on purpose, the few strands slipping loose are the only thing about her that doesn't look controlled.

There are piercings—silver hoops and a stud in her ears, and a small nose ring that catches the light when she turns her head. Not flashy. Just... her. Like everything about her was chosen with intention.

Ink peeks from under the edge of her top and along her forearm—black linework, clean and deliberate. A wildflower with thorns. A tiny dagger tucked behind her ear. Script I can't read from here, hidden like it's for her and no one else. The tattoos don't harden her; they underline her. Proof she's made decisions and lived through them.

Her boots are scuffed and the leather on her belt is worn in the places her hands land most. She looks like trouble and work ethic at the same time.

Then she lifts her gaze.

And those eyes pin me—cool, quiet, assessing. No warmth or welcome. Just claws tucked under calm, as though she's already decided I'm either a problem or a temporary inconvenience.

My brain does what it's trained to do: read

posture, distance, exits. But another part of me clocks the other tells—the tension in her jaw, the way she holds her shoulders like she's braced for impact that never comes.

Like someone who expects the world to swing first.

I smile anyway. Not big. Not pushy. Just… friendly. Like I don't notice she's daring me to flinch.

Mila clears her throat. "Lenni, this is Harlan Godfrey. Primary close protection starting tonight."

Lenni's gaze flicks to my badge, then back to my face. One corner of her mouth lifts—almost amused, like she already found the weakest point in the situation and plans to poke it until it bleeds.

I step forward just enough to be polite, not enough to crowd her. "Nice to meet you, Ms. Vale. Harlan Godfrey."

She scans me—boots to shoulders to face— then deadpans, "Nice to meet you, Hank."

Ah, a test.

My smile tugs wider before I can stop it. "It's Harland," I say, still warm.

Mila makes a low sound – half warning, half *good luck*.

Lenni leans back against the counter. "And I'm Lenni," she says, as if that bit is nonnegotiable.

The words come out kind enough, but there's a faint edge under them—rougher than the polish, like something she didn't bother sanding down.

"Lenni," I repeat, giving her the inch she demanded.

Her eyes narrow—annoyed that I didn't take the bait.

The door slams open and Rowan Kelly strolls in like trouble with eyeliner—jet-black hair, guitar strap slung over her shoulder, grin sharp enough to cut glass. She takes one look at me and looks delighted about it.

"Well," she drawls. "That's tragic."

Lenni's eyes spark just slightly. "Ro."

Rowan arches an eyebrow so high it threatens escape. "He's handsome." She jabs a finger at my chest like she's planting a flag. Reading my tag on my shirt, she whispers, "Harlan."

I lift my chin. "Rowan."

Lenni makes a quiet sound that might be a laugh and might be a threat.

Rowan closes the distance to just shy of rude. "So," she says, voice sweet as a barb, "are you the kind of bodyguard who's going to tell us what we can and can't do?"

I grin before curiosity kicks in. "I'm the kind who prefers everyone stays in one piece."

Her smile snaps wider, surprise flickering. "Fair enough."

Lenni watches us like she's bored – yet her stance says she's tuned in to every nuance.

Rowan shifts her gaze to Lenni. "You letting him call you *Ms. Vale* all tour? Because I'll puke."

Lenni keeps her eyes on me. "He can try."

I nod like I'm taking notes. "Roger that."

Rowan squints at me. "Why are you so... agreeable?"

I shrug, still smiling. "People who like me tend to survive. Less paperwork that way."

Lenni's lips twitch—she hates that its funny.

Mila's voice cuts in, flat as steel. "Ro, out. We hit the stage in ten."

Rowan throws up mock surrender. "Sure, sure."

At the door she pauses, eyes flicking back to me—all business this time. "Keep her upright," she says.

Not a question. More like a promise I can't break. I flash my friendliest mask. "Always."

She holds that gaze for a beat longer, then taps two fingers against her guitar strap out of habit, then storms down the hall.

Lenni's eyes remain locked on mine – cool, silent, measuring.

I keep it breezy. "So... Hank?"

Her lips curl. "Yeah. Hank it is."

I grin, dangerously smooth. "Alright. We'll put it on the list."

"The list?" she echoes, skeptical.

"Yeah," I say, easily. "The list of things you'll pretend don't make you laugh."

Her eyes narrow – irritated, maybe.

Or entertained.

Either way, she doesn't look away first.

And in that moment, I know: this tour just guaranteed its own kind of chaos.

And I'm not just watching for threats, I'm watching her.

At showtime, the venue hums with heat and bodies packed shoulder to shoulder. "*Barracuda*" by Heart rips through the speakers while we wait for Lenni's cue, the riff coiling the crowd tighter by the second.

Fans surge against the barricade like they're on a magnet's chain. Floor security adjusts – hands up, eyes sweeping, stance widening.

I take my spot just off-stage: pit in my sightline, side corridors covered, stage access locked down. Comms checked. Exits mapped.

Routine.

Then Lenni steps out— and the roar crashes over me like a wave. Even from here, she looks born for this moment. The crowd chants her name in rolling thunder.

She lifts the mic, flings them a line, and they answer with full-throttle volume. The band detonates into the first song, each musician locked in perfect sync.

The bassist and drummer create a foundation

so solid you could build skyscrapers on it. The lead guitarists fingers blur across the frets like she's channeling something holy.

They're not just good.

They're inevitable.

Lenni Vale is something else.

That's where it gets different. Plenty of artists shine under lights and slick production. But Lenni Vale…her voice has grit and warmth, like smoke laced with sunshine.

Then the lighting cue hits.

She eases into a soft line and the room falls silent, thousands of strangers frozen as if they've been waiting for a secret whisper.

Lenni steps forward alone, acoustic guitar in hand, her band fading back into shadow.

She owns the spotlight—controlled, self-assured, utterly in command.

I stay alert— scanning, counting, doing my job.

From my position offstage, the difference is obvious – my six-five frame built as a barrier, her five-two silhouette designed to ignite.

Then she lifts her chin, eyes skimming the crowd like she's counting bruises.

Not pity. Not softness.

Recognition.

Lenni taps twice over her heart—small, deliberate – and thousands of hands echo her gesture. My ribs tighten with that electric thrill.

Ro mirrors the motion a beat late, exaggerated, making Kai snort beside her. Lenni doesn't look back — but her shoulders loosen like she expected it.

Her mouth quirks—half smirk, half warning—and her voice carries, husky with that Tennessee-grit edge that makes people lean in like they're being let in on a secret.

"Hey," she says. "Don't get cute on me."

A ripple of laughter rolls through the room—relief disguised as noise.

Lenni points the mic toward the front row like she's choosing someone. Then another. Then the back, the shadows, the people who always try to disappear even while they're standing in a crowd.

"I see you," she says.

Three words. Sharp enough to cut. Gentle enough to save.

The audience reacts—not in raucous cheers, but in a collective exhale, like she just found the part of them they keep hidden and didn't ask permission to hold it.

Lenni's smile turns razor-thin. "Yeah. I do." She pauses like she's daring anyone to argue. "The ones who act tough. The ones who came alone. The ones who got dragged here and pretend they're too cool to care."

Her eyes flash, wicked and warm at the same time. "And the ones who've been carrying too much for too damn long."

Then her expression softens by a fraction, the

kind of softness you only get from someone who's survived enough to know it isn't a weakness.

Her voice drops. "The porch lights on, baby. I'm glad you came."

Something warm blooms in my chest.

Not attraction. Not yet. Recognition. Like watching someone build safety out of nothing but willpower.

She doesn't bask in it. Doesn't soak it up like attention.

She *claims* it—like she built this room into a shelter and everyone inside is under her protection for three minutes and twenty-seven seconds.

The first chord rings out—clean, acoustic, almost too tender for the way she usually bites. The amber porch-light glow hits her hair and makes her look like trouble in a church parking lot.

This isn't a flashy showcase.

It's a vow with teeth.

Her fingers move over the strings, steady and sure. Her voice drifts in, and the crowd leans forward like dogs answering a gentle whistle. It's a promise song. A safe haven song.

The others watch her differently than fans do — not dazzled, not worshipful.

Protective. Like they know the cost behind the performance.

And still—there's an edge threaded through

every line, like she's offering comfort but daring the world to try and take it from her.

Her lyrics spill out:

> *I'll leave the porch light burning for the ones who pace till dawn,*
> *For hearts that keep on running*
> *from nights they can't move on.*
> *Come as you are, come undone—*
> *I won't force you into confession.*
> *If you're tired of staying strong,*
> *There's room here for you to rest.*

She hits *confession* like it's a word she hates. Like she's spent a lifetime being forced into one.

A few rows back, someone sobs—quiet, ugly, relieved.

Lenni doesn't look away. She doesn't flinch. She lets them have it, lets them be seen, like crying in public is just another form of honesty.

And without looking at me, she finds where I'm standing anyway—or maybe I just feel found.

I've guarded the elite—the wealthy, beautiful, magnetic figures who bend every space around them. I've seen crowds scream for them, reporters swarm them, security cordon them off.

Yet none of them stirred anything in me.

But here, beneath that warm amber glow, I realize something uncomfortable:

She isn't drawing energy from them.

She's *giving it back.*

She knows what it costs to fill a room and still

feel alone. She's leaving a light burning in the dark, inviting everyone home—while keeping one hand wrapped around a knife, just in case.

Somewhere between the first verse and the chorus, I realize I'm no longer fixated on threats. My attention is on her—how her voice cracks at just the right moment, how her face stills when she means it, how she can make vulnerability feel like a dare.

I force myself back to the pit. Inhale through my nose. Widen my stance.

Professional.

But the impact is already lodged under my ribs, sharp and inconvenient.

Because I don't just want her safe now.

I want her protected from whatever taught her to sing like that.

When the song ends, the cheer surges—louder, brighter—and Lenni steps into it like she didn't just bare the softest piece of herself in front of strangers.

Like she didn't just hand them a porch light and a place to rest.

She taps her chest twice again—quick, like she's sealing it shut—and the crowd mirrors her like a vow.

I tighten my earpiece. Realign my focus, scan the exits once more.

Rules are rules.

My job is to keep her safe—

even if she's the first principal I've ever known

who makes a room feel safer simply by standing in it.

And that might be the most dangerous thing about her.

CHAPTER 3

Lennon

West Virginia

When I wake in West Virginia, the color of the world matches my mood more than I want to admit.

Gray sky. Gray roads. Gray mountains in the distance like someone sketched them in with a dull pencil and forgot to shade the rest.

Tour life isn't glamorous the way people think it is. It's not champagne and confetti and endless parties. It's pure adrenaline and sweat and a thousand hands grabbing at you through barricades and then—when the lights cut—it's bone-deep exhaustion.

Last night in Kentucky, I held it together on stage like always. Afterward, I smiled for the crew, thanked the venue, posed with Hollow Mesa because Mila said it was "good optics," then let Hank steer me back to the bus before my legs turned to jelly.

I told myself I allowed it because I was tired. Not because part of me liked having someone solid at my back.

Evie liked me best when I played dangerous. It made the story cleaner.

Once we were rolling, I squeezed into my

tiny bathroom—lukewarm water, shaking walls—and washed off sweat, eyeliner, and the last taste of fear. Then I threw on yoga pants and an oversized tee and tried to sleep. Grits shadowed me everywhere. He's small, stubborn, and convinced every unfamiliar sound is a threat.

Honestly, same.

When I step out of my room the next morning, the bus is quiet, and the bunks down the hall are dark. No Ro. No Kai. No Sin. Just the soft hum of the generator.

The kitchen lights glowed softly, and there was Hank, as if he lived here: black tee stretch across his chest, tactical pants, no badge but the authority lingered in his posture, broad shoulders nearly spanning the width of the booth.

His light hair is kept short at the sides, just enough on top to hint at a natural wave, his jaw roughened with the kind of three-day stubble that reads more "*I've been working doubles*" than "*I spent thirty minutes with a trimmer*." A faint scar bisects his right eyebrow—thin as a paper cut, old enough to have faded silver, not dramatic enough to ask about.

He looks like the type of man who'd help an old lady with her groceries in the rain and still mentally catalog every license plate in the parking lot on the way back to his car.

He looks up when I step into the light, eyes the color of bourbon catching the glow.

Not startled. Not curious.

Aware.

Like he's been tracking my presence since the second we boarded the bus, like he's been counting my footsteps all along.

My skin tightens at the instinct of being observed. Not because I'm scared. Because I don't like *being monitored*—even when the person doing it has good intentions and a face that belongs on a romance cover.

Especially then.

I noticed his bag on the bunk by the door—practical, defensive. He didn't pick it because it was comfortable. He picked it because it was a line of defense

I *should* hate that. I've handled myself this long. I've survived worse than a man with a radio and a hero complex.

But my annoyance... doesn't quite land. It just circles like a dog looking for a place to lie down.

Grits peeks around my leg, tail low. He stiffs when he sees Hank. Hank sets his coffee down, drops to one knee, and holds out his hand, palm down. No cooing. No claiming. "Hey, buddy. I'm not here to take your job," he said quietly.

Grits huffs, then edges forward. Hank stays still. Patient. Grits sniffs once, twice—wrist, jeans hem—then bumps his nose against Hank's knuckles.

Hank's lips twitch into what counts as a smile.

That's the thing about him – he doesn't push. He just exists, steady and open like he expects the best out of the world.

It makes *me* want to bite him.

My chest pinches. I clear my throat. "This is Grits."

"I figured," Hank says, eyes flicking to the dog.

"And this is Hank," I add. "He's... with us."

"With you," he corrects, still kneeling.

The nuance hits like a thumbprint on glass. Too intimate. Too *certain.*

Like he already decided what side he's on. "You're up early," I say, sidling to the coffee.

"I'm always up early."

I pour a mug, over-creamed it, and took a deep sip. "Did you sleep?"

"A little."

"West Virginia today."

He nods. "I saw the route."

"Always?" I tease.

"I see everything."

"Control freak."

"Safety measure."

I glance at his bunk. Grits presses against my leg. I stroke his ears, watching Hank over my mug. "You ever turn off the vigilance?" I ask.

"No. Not on assignment."

"Must be exhausting."

"It is." He pauses, then adds like it's nothing, "But it's part of the job."

I almost choke on my coffee. "Relax," I say instantly. "I'm not a fragile antique vase."

His mouth quirks. "Didn't say you were fragile."

"Mm-hmm." I eye him over my mug. "But you're thinking it."

"I'm thinking you're stubborn," he says, tone warm like it's a compliment.

I narrow my eyes. "Careful, Hank. Compliments make me feral."

"Noted," he says, like he's collecting little facts the way he collects exits.

He rises, easy and unhurried, and Grits—traitor—leans toward him like he's been waiting for permission

Hank scratches behind Grits's ear like he's known him forever. "Good man," he murmurs. "Keeping watch."

Grits' tail gives a cautious thump.

My pride hates the sight. My body... doesn't.

"I've got a soft spot for West Virginia," I say, because talking is easier than admitting anything else.

"Because it's close to home?" he asks.

"Because it's honest," I say. "It doesn't pretend."

He nods, as if he understood exactly.

Grits curls at my feet, finally relaxed. Maybe the nicest thing that happened out here all day.

Silence falls—comfortable, functional.

Somewhere down the hall, the band stirs in their bunks. The bus groans. The world keeps moving.

He sips his coffee, glances at the corridor, then

back at me as naturally as blinking.

That's the danger. Not the broad shoulders or the husky voice.

The steady. The golden. The way my nervous system recognizes him as sunlight.

My shoulders drop before I can stop them.

I hate that.

Easy is how people get hurt.

I look away first, irritated that I even noticed—that "safe" has a shape, and it's wearing a black T-shirt five feet from me.

My eyes drift to the counter: two protein bars, a neat stack of paper cups, a hand towel folded too perfectly.

Every crease aligned—Hank's signature, like disorder is an enemy he can eradicate.

And for one treasonous second, I wonder what it would feel like… to let him.

I'm still smiling when the first bunk curtain whips open.

Ro emerges like a gremlin summoned by caffeine—hair a wreck, eyeliner smudged like she slept face-first into a pillowcase, wearing giant basketball shorts and a hoodie that absolutely cost more than my first car but looks like it was stolen from a 2009 boyfriend.

She stops when she sees Hank, then she looks at me, then back to him,

Her mouth curls – pure menace, pure delight. Like she just found a new hobby and it's making me uncomfortable.

"Well," she rasps, voice rough with sleep, "look who's up. Officer Golden."

Hank chokes on his coffee. "Not an officer."

Ro strides into the kitchenette, snatches one of his protein bar, and drops into the seat across from him.

He doesn't budge, doesn't even look mildly inconvenienced. Ro squints at him like a cat deciding whether to knock a glass off the counter.

He meets her stare without challenge or retreat.

The next curtain peels back gently.

Kai slips out, soft-footed—sleep-tousled blonde hair, bare face, eyes already sharp as if she sleeps with one ear open. She nods at me—no words needed—then turns to Hank. She doesn't smile or frown, just measures him: posture, stance, hands. Their gazes lock for a long second and the air gets colder.

Kai dips her chin. "Morning."

"Morning," Hank says.

No charm. No extra. Two professionals acknowledging each other.

Ro beams. "Great—two robots. Perfect."

Kai reaches for a mug. "Coffee?"

"Fresh," Hank answers, and she pours in silence.

Then the final curtain snaps wide.

Sin appears—red hair wild, tank and sweats, tattoos traced in shadow. She sizes up Hank in a heartbeat, edge in her look.

"Who's this, again?" she asks, low.

"Primary protection," I say before he can.

Sin narrows her eyes. "He looks like a drill sergeant."

Ro snickers. "Basically."

Hank remains unmoved, meeting Sin's stare with the same calm neutrality. She crouches to scratch Grits behind the ears.

"Dog likes you?" she asks.

Grits yawns.

Hank's mouth tips into something that counts as a smile. "Seems so."

Sin's mouth tilts—something close to approval. "Interesting."

Ro leans forward, stage-whispering. "So, Hank—"

"It's Harlan," he corrects, cool and immediate.

Ro grins like she lives for corrections.

"Right, *Harlan*. How long are we stuck with you?"

His gaze never wavers. "As long as I'm needed."

Ro glances at me, then back. "And what decides that?"

Hank's voice is steady: "When the threats end."

My stomach twists.

Ro's grin falters.

Because we all heard it. Not *if – when*.

Kai's hand lands on my shoulder, brief and grounding. Her silence message: *we've got you.*

Sin sit settles next to Ro, still studying Hank.

"How'd you scare the dog into being brave?"

Hank quirks a half-smile—barely there, but real. "My charming personality."

I blink.

Ro loses it, laughing so hard she has to brace a hand on the table like she might slide right off the bench.

Hank's gaze flicks to me over his coffee, expression neutral—professional mask locked in.

I hate that it makes my mouth twitch.

For a moment, with my band half-awake and my dog no longer trembling and the smell of coffee in the air, it almost feels normal.

Almost.

Then the front door of the bus crashes open, cool morning air blasting in.

Mila Santos storms through like a general. "Rise and shine. Load-in at eleven. Meet-and-greet at four. Soundcheck at five-thirty. Lenni, local radio at two. Ro, Kai, Sin—wardrobe with Tessa in thirty."

She swivels to Hank. "Godfrey. Walkthrough in ten."

"Yes, ma'am."

Then Mila looks at me – measured, surgical. "Lenni," she says, "we keep it tight. We keep it clean."

Translation: no mistakes, no cracks, no headlines we didn't approve.

I swallow down the dread trying to climb my throat. "Let's do it," I say on instinct.

Mila nods once—no smile—and strides off, radio crackling.

Silence falls. Ro bangs her head gently on the table. "She's going to kill us."

Kai sips her coffee, calm as ever. "Probably."

Harlan stands, efficient, already heading forward as if pulled by Mila's orders. He pauses, glances back at me—professional pose, controlled calm—but his eyes hold mine a beat too long. A reminder: he's here, whether I want him or not.

Whether I need him or not.

I wrap my fingers around my warm mug and stare out at the gray West Virginia ridges – honest, unforgiving, beautiful without permission.

And against my will I think: if Hank's going to share my space, I'll have to choose which walls stay up... and which ones I let him sit beside without baring my teeth.

CHAPTER 4

Harlan

Virginia

It's the last show on this run of dates before a short pause.

We're in Virginia – close enough to home that I can taste it when I breathe. Close enough that my sister would come unglued if she knew exactly what town we were in tonight.

Since it's the last show of this leg, there's no overnight haul once the encore ends. No engines roaring to life the second the last note fades. No driver guzzling coffee while everyone pretends one bad merge won't send them off the road.

That shift changes the vibe. The crowd drifts out at its own pace. The crew doesn't sprint. People linger in halls as if they have nowhere to be except wherever they want.

And that's when mistakes happen.

I settle where I always do—close enough to keep her in view, far enough not to crowd her. I watch the exits, the staff-only doors, anyone who seems too interested.

Lenni steps offstage drenched in sweat and adrenaline; leather and denim still sculpt her into something larger than the room.

She flashes the crew a smile, thanks the venue

manager, takes a bottle of water from Harper while Tess straightens a strap.

It looks effortless.

But it isn't.

Tonight she's laughing—genuine bursts of joy between the after-show shuffle, as if she's letting herself savor the victory before locking it down again.

And it hits me how rare that is. How controlled she usually stays. How hard she must fight to let her feel anything unscripted.

"Lennaayyyy!"

Colby Bridges' voice drawls through the corridor, stretched out like Texas highway. Lead singer of Hollow Mesa: tall and fit, curly blonde hair under a cap. His smile spreads slow as honey, all camera-ready charm.

"Y'all got a minute?" he calls, each syllable riding longer than it needs to. He doesn't just like attention – he feeds on it like barbecue at a family reunion.

He strides over, beer in hand, eyes bright with that post-show buzz. "Party at the hotel," he says. "Whole crew's coming—both bands. You gotta come celebrate. Last night of the leg."

Lenni flips on her smile—easy, flirty, armor polished to a mirror shine. The kind of smile that keeps men entertained while she counts the steps to the nearest exit.

"Do I gotta?" she teases, voice sweet, eyes sharp.

Colby laughs, tipping his beer toward her like a toast. "Yes ma'am. You're the headliner. It's basically your civic duty."

Behind him, Ro stands with arms crossed, amused at his effort. Kai and Sin hover near Lenni – loose, casual, but positioned like they'd bite first and apologize later. At the far end, Mila watches like a hawk in human form.

Colby's gaze shifts to me—brief, calculating. His grin sharpens. "And your... guy," he nods toward me, "he gonna tag along?"

I don't blink. I let Lenni handle it.

Her eyes flick to mine for a heartbeat – not permission or reassurance. A systems check.

"Yeah," she says, sweet as poison. "He goes wherever I go."

Something tight in my chest loosens – and I hate that I notice.

Colby's laugh stutters; he recovers with a practiced smoothness that speaks of Austin open mics. "Right. Yeah. Of course. Just... didn't know if he—"

"He does," Lenni cuts in, smile never slipping. Her brand face stays on, but the message underneath is all teeth.

Colby lifts his hands in mock surrender. "Okay, okay. Don't shoot me."

I offer a mild, harmless smile. "I'm a lover, not a shooter."

Lenni's grin widens like she's enjoying the lie. "Don't let him fool you, Colby. He's fun at parties."

Colby's brows lift, attention snagging again. "Yeah?"

"Thrilling," Lenni replies, voice smooth as whiskey. "He stands in corners and judges people's life choices."

"Only the unsafe ones," I add, easy.

Colby clears his throat and rolls his shoulders like he's putting his swagger back on. "Hotel in an hour. Don't bail on us."

Lenni tilts her head, lashes lowering – all stage, all control, all calculated charm. "Wouldn't dream of it."

The hotel bar throbs with that staged energy —music cranked too bright, lights sunk too low, bodies packed too tight.

Crews fill tables, both bands spread out like armies, laughter pinging against phone screens and rows of drinks lining the counters.

Lenni sweeps in and everything shifts.

Not loudly or dramatically. Just gravity recalibrating around her.

She's still in full post-show mode, lipstick smudged into that perfect hint of chaos. Trouble that sells tickets.

The security team and I take our positions—I angle myself with the bar to my left, the main entrance visible from the corner of my eye, and the mirror behind the liquor shelves reflecting any movement I might miss. I keep my stance loose, approachable, even while my gut knots tighter every time she laughs.

Because it feels too easy to forget she isn't mine to watch that way.

Colby spots her and barrels over, charm dialed to eleven—drawl thick as molasses, grin wide enough to catch headlights—and offers her a beer like it's an invitation only she can accept.

She lifts the bottle, wraps her fingers around it just so, takes one small, deliberate sip, then lowers it again. Colby either doesn't notice or chooses not to.

He leans in, voice low, and she tosses back a bright laugh—head tipped, eyes lit—loud enough to be heard, light enough to keep him from leaning closer.

Anyone watching would swear it's flirting. Anyone paying attention would see the space she never gives up.

She brushes his shoulder in passing – light as a ghost – then steps away before the moment weighs real. Touch offered.

Access denied.

My jaw tightens. Jealousy slides in slow and unwelcome – sharp enough to notice, subtle enough to deny.

The opening notes of "Shut Up and Dance" by WALK THE MOON blast through the speakers, and suddenly Clint – Hollow Mesa's drummer – has her by the fingertips, spinning her toward the dance floor.

The gold band on his finger glints under the lights – all fun, no subtext.

Lenni surrenders to the rhythm, hips rolling on cue, smiling like she owns the room. Cell phones pop up, punctuated by sharp whistles of appreciation.

Across the floor Ro leans into Hollow's guitarist, Blaize, her eyelashes fluttering as she whispers something in his ear. His responding smile suggest they're co-conspirators in some mischief.

I stay relaxed, nod to the bartender when he offers me water instead of whiskey. "Yeah," I tell him. "Two."

Colby hustles Lenni another beer before she's even halfway through the first.

"You need another one," he says, flashing that camera grin.

She takes it—because saying no would be a conversation—and sets it on the nearest table untouched. A prop, not a promise. Dances again, subtle, controlled, enough so he thinks he's winning.

My jaw clenches. I hate how tight that feels. I hate that it's jealousy, raw and unfiltered, and there's nothing in my contract to fix it.

Colby's slips a hand toward her waist; Lenni spins free, keeps it playful. He laughs, but I see the flicker – restless, wanting more.

She counteroffers with choreography, every gesture measured, every glance calibrated.

She doesn't look guilty. She looks like she's checking my corner, making sure I'm still there.

I lift one of the waters in a small, casual "you good?" gesture – nothing dramatic.

Her brows dip, annoyed that I clocked it so fast. Then she picks it up anyway.

Beer to water – Colby doesn't spot the swap, too busy watching himself in her attention.

He leans in again, low voice thick: "Gonna leave us tonight, Vale?" It's the last show. Live a little."

Lenni lets out that soft, well-practiced laugh and dips a tiny sip of beer to keep the act alive, then sets it down. "I did live," she says, voice cool. "I just did it onstage."

Then she sets it down.

Colby's grin wobbles. "Well, damn. Okay."

She ducks away from him and walks straight to me—steady footing, no stumble, no sway. No apology and no explanation.

"Ready?" she asks – directed at him.

Not the room, me.

The realization hits like a misstep – subtle and dangerous – and I shove it away before it can mean anything.

I blink once. "Yeah."

Her brow arches. "No ma'am?"

I grin. "Trying something new. Not getting murdered by your guitarist."

From behind, Ro's low cackle drifts over – flirting turned villainy.

Lenni's mouth tugs like she wants to smile but refuses.

We weave through the crowd, past the laughter and the music, through the noise people cling to for freedom.

Colby calls after her, half-joke, half-plea: "You really leaving with your bodyguard?"

Lenni doesn't look back. She lifts a lazy wave. "Yep."

We reach the elevator. The doors slide closed, cutting off the noise.

Silence drops like a curtain.

Lenni leans back against the wall for the brief ride up, eyes on the numbers, jaw set. The jokes are gone. The awareness isn't.

I don't ask if she's okay. I don't force softness out of her like it's owed to me. I just stand there – present, steady – like a guardrail you don't notice until you need it.

The elevator chimes.

We step out.

At Lenni's door, she swipes her keycard the lock flashes green.

Before she moves inside, I shift forward—steady, unhurried. Routine keeps you alive in this line of work.

"I'm going in first," I say.

Lenni's mouth curves – pure mischief – like she's already plotting how to make me regret this. She steps back a half-pace and lets me cross the threshold.

"Try not to find my embarrassing stuff," she says, too casual to be believable.

I arch a brow. "Define embarrassing."

She leans in just a fraction, "if you find my smutty books—don't read the highlighted parts."

I pause mid-step. "Highlighted?"

She shrugs like it's nothing. Like she's daring me to remember she controls this room. "I'm a dedicated reader."

"Uh-huh."

Lenni's smile goes slow. Wicked. "And if you find a toy... no you didn't."

My throat works once.

She watches it happen, delighted. "Oh," she murmurs, satisfied as hell. "There it is."

"There what?" I ask, because I'm an idiot.

"The moment you remember I'm not just a job," she says, voice soft as a threat. "You're blushing, Hank."

"I don't blush."

"You do," she says, smug. "It's adorable."

I exhale through my nose, fighting a grin. "I'm going to pretend none of this is happening."

Lenni's eyes gleam. "Good," she says. "Because I'll absolutely keep making it worse."

I sweep the room. Hotel rooms are all the

same: too many mirrors, too many hidden corners. Bathroom. Behind the shower curtain. Closet. Under the bed. Windows bolted. Latch. Deadbolt. No movement. No signs of tampering. Satisfied, I return to the main area.

Lenni leans against the entryway, arms folded, casual but watchful— like she's memorizing every step I take.

"You always gonna do that?" she asks.

"Yes."

"And if you found someone?"

"I wouldn't be having this conversation."

A flicker of something—humor or respect—crosses her face, then vanishes. She steps fully inside, kicks off her boots by the dresser, drops her leather jacket onto a chair, loosens her hair as the night's tension falls away. She looks younger then—never innocent, just… human.

I keep moving, finishing my sweep with the same calm I use everywhere. When I'm done, I glance back at her, deadpan.

"Good news," I say. "I didn't locate any suspicious persons, weapons, or—" my eyes flick to the dresser like I'm logging evidence "—toys."

Her mouth twitches. "Wow. So thorough."

"Extremely," I agree. "Only contraband I found was an attitude."

She huffs a laugh, quick and unwilling, then catches herself like laughter is a weakness.

I nod toward the kitchen. "Water's on the counter."

She glances over, notices the bottle, says nothing.

My voice drops lower. Business-like, safer. "Your room is next to mine. Deadbolt this door. Don't let anyone in—staff included—unless you check with me first. Need anything? Call my cell."

Lenni nods once, steady. No argument.

Then, quick and almost embarrassed by how natural it feels, she taps two fingers over her heart—the same signal she gives the crowd, now just for me. A silent *thank- you* she can't put into words.

She doesn't know what that gesture does to people. Doesn't know she hands out pieces of trust like they cost her something.

And I decide — without meaning to — that I won't be another person who wastes it.

She backs toward the bed, eyes still on me.

"Goodnight, Hank,"

"It's Harlan," I correct automatically.

She smiles—small, tired, real. "Sure it is." Then she slips into the bathroom and the door clicks shut.

I close her door behind me until it latches. I linger, staring at the wood grain like it's going to give me a lecture. It doesn't.

From the other side, I hear the soft rush of water as the shower turns on. My brain does something wildly unhelpful, like it hasn't already caused enough problems on this tour.

I exhale through my nose and force my feet to

move away from the door.

My room smells like hotel detergent and stale AC. I check my own windows out of habit, and send then my phone buzzes.

Lenni: *Did you actually check under the bed?*

I stare at the message.

I type back: *Yes.*

Lenni: *Liar*.

My mouth twitches.

Me: *I checked under the bed. Not even your patience could fit under there.*

Three dots appear. Disappear. Appear again.

Lenni: *I think I've been pretty patient for someone that has a full time shadow.*
Harlan: *at least the shadow is good looking.*
Lenni*: Don't push it, guidance counselor.*
Harlan: *Copy that.*

I drop the phone onto the couch by the door that connects our rooms, then start arranging the blankets.

A small sound from the door makes me go still. Not danger. Just... paws scratching.

I open the door a crack.

Grits stands there, ears perked, tail doing a cautious little wag like he's negotiating terms.

"Hey, buddy," I whisper, crouching.

He sniffs my shin, then trots past me. He circles once—tight, decisive—and hops up on the couch with a huff.

Then he looks at me like: *Well?*

I blink. "You're making yourself at home."

Grits' eyes half-close.

"Yeah," I mutter. "Me too."

I sit at the far end of the couch, leaving him his space. He immediately shuffles closer until his warm little body presses against my thigh like a claim. Protective. Loyal.

And because the universe has a sick sense of humor, he sighs—content—and my phone buzzes again.

Lenni: *Did you steal my dog?*

I glance at the dog. Then type: *He chose his team.*

Lenni: *He's food-motivated. You look like the type that packed beef jerky. Don't get cocky.*

Harlan: *I'm never cocky. I'm responsibly confident.*

Lenni: *Same thing.*

I can practically hear her voice in the words —sharp to cover soft. Claws out even when she's safe enough to text me from the other side of a wall.

I stare at the screen too long.

Then I set the phone face down like it might catch fire.

The wall between us might as well be paper. A drawer scrapes open. Then – vibrations pulse through the drywall, each one hammering into my chest.

I hear everything.

Her moans crack the silence. Not theatrical. Raw. Fractured at the edges like she's fighting against her own surrender and losing.

My throat goes tight.

Fuck.

I drill my eyes into the ceiling like it's salvation itself. Like control is a physical thing I can strangle if I just focus hard enough.

Like I'm not a man forged in discipline who's now coming apart because of a woman separated by three inches of nothing.

I shift on the couch, rip the blanket higher, and twist my body toward the door.

Like a locked entry point is what threatened me and not how my blood ignites at the sound of her release – first a whisper, then a demand, her pleasure climbing like a fever.

I drag oxygen through clinched teeth.

Because my contract is iron law.

And because craving her doesn't entitle me to a goddamn thing.

Grits noses my hand like he can feel my heart trying to escape my chest. He forces his head beneath my palm offering an anchor.

I pet him. Slow. Steady. A deliberate return to earth.

Minutes pass. The building settles. Virginia traffic hums outside.

But inside, her sounds brand themselves into my memory—brutal evidence that beneath her armor beats something wild, proof that she fractures when no one's watching.

And damning proof that I'm one heartbeat away from shattering the only rule that matters.

My phone lights up once more and I refuse to look—because the truth is already carved into my bones:

The contract is just ink.

The chemistry is wildfire.

And Lennon Vale can dominate an arena, stride away untouchable.. yet leave me destroyed like this – starving.

Not because she offered anything.

Because she took everything without touching me at all.

CHAPTER 5

Lennon

Tennessee

The streets of Nashville are familiar in a way that makes my guard want to drop – and my pride want to shove it right back up.

It's quiet in that expensive, manufactured way—thick glass, soundproof doors, city lights spread out like glitter.

Not home. Not comfort. A controlled pause.

I bought my mama a place before I ever bought myself anything permanent.

She needed roots.

I needed something I could leave without guilt. A place that didn't ask me to settle when my life never stopped moving.

This was supposed to feel like freedom.

Instead, it's just a different kind of cage – one with better locks and a better view.

They put Hank in the condo next door.

Not down the hall or on another floor—literally sharing a wall with me.

"Isn't that convenient?" Harper had chirped.

"Smart security move," Evie nodded. "Temporary," she added, smiling like it was reassurance instead of a threat.

"Non-negotiable," Mila had declared before I

could protest.

And Hank—Harlan, whatever—didn't say anything at all. He just stood there, solid as a redwood, eyes steady as if he wasn't completely upending my existence.

And somehow the silence was worse than arguments would've been. No pressure. No push. Just inevitability.

Credit where it's due: he gives me space.

He doesn't hover. Not handing out rulebooks or lectures. He just silently patrols—checking hallways, exits, and perimeters.

Then he vanishes into his own space. The perfect neighbor with a gun and muscles.

And somehow that's worse.

If he were controlling, I could rebel.

If he were a jerk, I could dismiss him.

But he's just... there. Like Chris Hemsworth on payroll.

Not trying to cage me in—trying to keep danger out.

And my body hums at his presence in ways I refuse to name.

I label it annoyance.

I've always been good at lying to myself.

Tonight I'm doing a late-night TV spot.

Sounds glamorous, doesn't it? Until you're in the thick of it.

It's orchestrated mayhem: stylists fussing with hair and makeup, wardrobe racks clattering, cameras swiveling, security on alert, producers with headsets and espresso breath buzzing around, stage managers barking countdowns like they're defusing a bomb. Everyone's moving too fast, grinning too wide, acting like this is normal.

I'm the guest – and the product.

My dressing room they give me is nicer than half the places I lived in growing up: plus couch, lighted vanity, a clothing rail flexing under outfits, water bottles lined up as through hydration alone could cure nerves.

Tess is already sorting garment bags, fingers flying, eyes sharp. Harper perches by the door with a clipboard, face so taut she might pass out if I sneeze wrong.

Evie scrolls her phone, polished and deadly serious, issuing orders like "Nope, skip that shot," and "Yes, she'll do it," as if I'm not sitting right here.

She never asks. She informs. Like the decision already happened somewhere above my head.

Ro, Kai, and Sin slip in behind me like a living barricade.

Ro radiates menace and dark humor, pacing as if she's itching to pick a fight.

Kai stands silent, eyes scanning every corner the way she reads a crowd when the pit gets too tight.

Sin leans by the window, arms crossed, daring anyone to get within biting distance.

My crew. My backbone.

I slide into my outfit—denim and leather, a mix of country grit and rock bite, armor sharp enough to keep the world at bay. My makeup is the usual: smoky lids, liner like a razor, lips stained like a warning.

Tess steps back, nods approvingly. "That's it. Perfect."

Harper bounces on her toes. "You look… insane."

"Exactly," I grin.

"Don't say anything off-script," Evie warns.

I lift a brow. "You mean don't tell America to kiss my—"

Evie's smile doesn't waver, like she's promising consequences. "Don't," she says softly.

Ro snorts. "Let her. It'll trend."

Kai whispers, "Please don't."

Sin says nothing, but her glare promises she'll drag me back by my ponytail if I try.

I roll my shoulders once, shedding tension like old skin.

A soft knock – two quiet taps – and a stage PA slips in. "Two minutes."

My stomach lurches. I don't flinch. Every nerve on edge, face like stone.

In my boots I stomp down the corridor toward the stage.

The studio is blinding—white-hot lights, reflective floors, an illusion of safety.

Band in place. Cameras sweeping. The host beams my name, the crowd roars as though we're old friends. Then the music drops.

I become Lenni Vale.

Leather and edge, raw power wrapped in a chorus.

My voice locks in. The band is razor-tight. The sound is clean, controlled – electricity engineered.

I can't see past the first rows, but I feel the crowd. Their focus. Their hunger. It presses in.

I keep my chin high, my gaze steady, serving up the smirk, the steel, the wicked edge they came for.

First verse sails by. The chorus hits.
Halfway through verse two, a flicker at stage right—by the barrier separating me from the audience.

A blur. A surge. Somebody lunges.

My blood freezes.

In a heartbeat, a fan's onstage. Security reacts too slowly, caught between rules and shock.

Hank doesn't hesitate.

He appears like it's just another Tuesday—no panic, no theatrics.

He doesn't tackle or slam. He steadies the fan with one firm hand on their shoulder, the other bracing them, guiding them back without turning it into a spectacle.

He murmurs something I can't catch over the music. The fan flails, still reaching.

Hank adjusts, steers them away as if escorting a drunk cousin out of a wedding.

The moment dissolves. Cameras keep rolling.

The crowd gasps, then cheers—danger as entertainment when it isn't happening to them.

My lips keep moving. My body keeps performing. Meanwhile, my lungs... forget how.

I finish the song—professionalism and fear of shattering propel me to the end.

Final note. Thunderous applause.

The host beams, "LENNI VALE!"

I flash the practiced smile, wave, nod.

Backstage, my hands tremble as I step off.

Not a collapse. Not a dramatic faint. Just a subtle betrayal—knees loose, breath skidding shallow, air thinning like someone quietly turned down the oxygen. My ribs lock tight, cinched like a belt pulled one notch too far.

I hate that anyone can see it.

If I look in control, I am in control. That's the rule. Always has been.

Harper's there instantly, eyes wide.

"Lenni—"

"Don't."

The word snaps out sharp, reflexive.

If she asks if I'm okay, I'll shatter. And if I shatter, someone will film it. Someone will spin it. Someone will own it.

Ro clocks me from across the hall, expression hardening. She knows the difference between adrenaline and panic—has since Slateford, since we were two girls clawing our way out of the same nowhere town with nothing but borrowed amps and stubborn hope.

She followed me to Nashville chasing this dream, slept on floors beside me, sang backup when I couldn't afford a band, stood behind me onstage long before anyone knew my name.

Ro has always been my echo and my shield.

"What the hell was that?" she demands.

Kai's jaw is tight—anger or leftover adrenaline, I can't tell. Sin's already moving, body angled outward, scanning the hallway like she's deciding who she'd take down first if given the chance.

Evie strides in, phone already out. Her heels hit the floor like a countdown.

"We'll call it enthusiastic, not a breach—"

She doesn't ask if I'm hurt, or if I'm scared. She looks at me like the chaos is my fault for existing.

"Mila," I cut in, voice taut.

Mila appears immediately, summoned by tone alone. Her gaze is steel. "He's secured. Studio security has him in custody."

My heart won't slow. My breathing won't calm. It's like I'm still onstage, still feeling them pushing at me.

Then Hank steps into view.

Not rushing, not barking orders—just there.

Relaxed stance. Calm face. A presence so steady my body recognizes it before my brain does. My breathing stutters—then, traitorously, eases. Like my system has been waiting for visual confirmation that it's over.

"Lenni," he says quietly, no pressure.

The room keeps talking—Evie, Mila, Ro, Sin blocking half the hallway without breaking conversation—but it all blurs into static when his voice says my name. I turn toward him, dragging my expression back into place.

"You show up like a magic trick now?"

He quirks a corner of his mouth. "Overachieving."

It's dumb, half a joke, and it cracks something open anyway.

Evie presses on. "We'll post a clip. We'll control the narrative. Lenni, just say the fans got carried away—" Her tone tightens on my name, a warning disguised as guidance.

I lift a hand. "Everyone out." The accent that slips loose isn't sweet – more Tennessee whiskey than honey, rough around the edges and harder to ignore.

Evie blinks. "Excuse me?" Not confused – offended. Like I just broke protocol.

I repeat, flat: "Out."

Ro arches a brow, amused. She's the only one who can laugh right now, because Ro's always been the bridge between "Lenni Vale" and "Lennon who might actually fall apart." And she knows that when my vowels go sharp, it's not a performance. It's a warning.

Kai's eyes soften. Sin looks relieved to have direction. Mila steps smoothly between Evie and me. "Five minutes. Clear out."

Evie's lips thin into a smile that doesn't reach her eyes. She doesn't move right away – just lets the pause stretch, like she's reminding me who usually wins these standoffs. Then she clicks away in her heels.

Harper hesitates, then bolts like she's remembered the stove's on. Ro lingers, smirking at Hank. "Don't get weird, cop."

"I'm not a cop," he says automatically.

"Sure, Hank," she teases—then her expression flicks to me for half a beat – quick, private. The look that says: *I'm here. I'm not leaving. Breathe.* Then she goes.

I stand in the middle of the dressing room, fists clenched, jaw aching. Hank stays near the door, not crowding me. Giving me the dignity of space.

"You didn't freak out," I say, because the words have to go somewhere.

He shrugs. "There wasn't time."

"People storming the stage on live TV isn't... normal."

"No," he agrees softly. "It's not."

I swallow, forcing my breathing to even out through sheer stubbornness. "And yet you looked like you were taking out the trash."

"I've taken out trash before."

A laugh escapes me before I can stop it.

I hate how much I need that right now.

I hate more that my body settles when he's here.

I swallow it down fast — because needing someone else to hold the line has never ended well for me.

"Why does this keep happening?" I blurt – too honest, too soft. Regret flares instantly. Soft gets mistaken for permission. Soft gets your comments you never asked for – a hand lingering too long, a "smile for me" from men with power and money, men saying things he shouldn't have said to a little girl who still slept with a nightlight. I learned early what men take when you look breakable.

Hank doesn't pounce. He doesn't pry. He steps a bit closer, careful, respectful. "We don't know yet," he says. "But we will."

I give a humorless laugh. "You're so… confident."

"It's my job."

That line again—his shield. But with him, it lands like a promise, not a wall. And that pisses me off, too. Because my body believes him before my brain can argue.

My breathing finally evens out. I drag a hand through my hair, yanking my ponytail tighter like I can pull myself back together.

"I hate this."

"I know."

No platitudes. No fixes. Just *I know*. It settles heavy and warm in my chest. I'm angry at that warmth. Angry at myself for wanting it. I've been my own protection for so long my instincts don't know what to do with a man who doesn't try to cash in on my fear.

I stare at him—broad shoulders, calm eyes, a man who stands close enough to shelter me without trying to consume me. And the realization hits me harder than the scare did: I don't want him to leave. I should. I absolutely should. But I don't.

Not because I want him. Because I want what he is in this moment: a lock that walks. A body between me and the world.

"Can you.. just – " The words stumble. I hate that I have to say them. hate that my throat tightens like I'm asking for something I'm not allowed to want.

He waits patiently. Damn him.

"I want you to sleep on my couch," I blurt, like ripping off a bandage. "Tonight. Just— in case." "Couch," I add fast. "Door locked. No talking… this isn't.. that." I don't even know what that is supposed to mean – only that I refuse to hand him anything soft enough to be misunderstood.

Silence stretches as my face heats. "And before you get a big head—"

"Already got one."

"Harlan."

He lifts a hand, still gentle. "Okay."

No teasing, no triumph. Just acceptance. Like I asked him to pass the salt instead of guard my sleep. Like he understands this is a safety plan, not an invitation.

Relief crashes through me. I turn away, smoothing my jacket so I don't have to look at him. I can't believe I needed him – and he didn't gloat. Didn't smirk like I'd finally cracked. Didn't look at me like a prize.

"I'm not freaked out," I mutter.

"I know."

I scoff. "You don't know anything."

A slow, patient smile. "Okay. I do know you're breathing like you just ran a mile."

"I'm fine."

"Sure." He tilts his head. "You want space – or you want me to guard the door and shoo everyone else off?"

My throat tightens. "…Guard the door."

Not comfort. Not closeness. Just a boundary I don't have to hold alone.

"Copy that." Simple and professional, and somehow it rearranged everything.

"You're gonna tell Mila?" I ask.

"For safety."

"I hate you."

His eyes soften. "Yeah. You don't."

It lands like a challenge. Like he's reading my tells, mapping the places I keep locked down. Like he can see a difference between desire and survival – and he's not confusing them.

I should shut this off. Joke it away. Leave first.

But my breathing is steady now.

And that's the problem.

CHAPTER 6

Harlan

Tennessee

I pause at her door, sweeping the corridor—left, right, the ceiling corner where the camera perches. No one loiters, no doors ajar, no movement on the stairwell.

I listen anyway. Silence is just a room holding its breath.

I rap once and the door opens a sliver. Lenni's face appears — hair piled messily, eyeliner still clinging from the show. She glances at my bag, then at me, already irritated I followed her instructions so literally.

"You travel light," she says, amusement in her tone. The joke lands easy, but her eyes don't soften.

She steps aside and I slip in.

My eyes flick over the room, mapping it instinctively.

Lenni shuts the door, locks it, and leans against it like she's bracing for instructions.

I don't give any.

I drop my duffel by the couch and head straight to the windows.

"Seriously?" she asks.

"Seriously."

She trails behind – arms folded, feigning annoyance – but her eyes track the same details mine do: balcony latch, window locks, the thin seam of the sliding door.

She's pretending she's humoring me.

She's not.

She's checking too.

And she doesn't even realize she does it.

A familiar scuff of nails hits the tile behind me —confident, not cautious.

"Hey, buddy," I say without turning, because I already know who it is.

Grits trots down the hallway like he owns the place, tail up and ears perked—still grumpy-faced, still judging, but no longer acting like I'm a stranger. He stops at my heel and bumps my ankle with his nose.

"Yeah," Lenni mutters behind me. "He's decided you're… acceptable."

"High praise," I say.

Grits sniffs my duffel, then flops onto the rug with a dramatic sigh—right in my path, the way he does on the bus when he wants attention but refuses to ask for it.

I crouch and scratch behind his ears. His eyes half-close immediately, leaning into my hand.

"There's my guy," I murmur.

Lenni makes a sound that could be annoyance or affection, hard to tell with her.

"Don't let it go to your head."

I straighten and go back to business, checking

the bedroom and bathroom window locks.

When I finish, I return to the living room.

"Okay," I say. "It's secure."

She lifts an eyebrow. "Congratulations."

"Thank you."

Her stern mask falters – almost a smile – before snapping back into place.

She disappears down the hall and then reappears with a pillow and folded blankets.

"There," she says. "So you don't… suffer."

"I do appreciate that."

Her gaze flicks away, too quickly for it to be casual.

"Don't make it weird."

"I'm physically incapable of making anything weird."

She lets out a sharp, surprised laugh, as though her own body betrayed her. Then she clamps it down like laughter is a loose thread.

Every time she laughs, it feels like she didn't mean to let me see that version of her.

I unfold the blanket and drape it over the couch carefully, earning a skeptical squint from her.

"There," I say. "Your couch remains unharmed."

"My couch was never the concern," she replies. Too quick. Too flat.

I hold her gaze. "No?"

She meets my eyes for half a beat—cool, unblinking—then turns away, masking the crack she just revealed.

She steps into the kitchen, swings open the fridge door, and peers inside as if the answers are on a shelf.

"You hungry?" she asks, casual.

"Are you?" I shoot back.

She hesitates. "I asked first."

The hesitation is barely there — just a fraction too long — like she has to check with her own body before answering.

"I could eat."

She sighs. "I didn't buy food. Harper stocked me with sparkling water and yogurt."

"Figures."

She scowls, grabs a water bottle, twists the cap as if it's offended her, takes a swig, then lifts her phone toward me.

"Want to order something?" she says too casually.

Her voice stays light, but her shoulders dip the second she thinks I'm not looking — like the effort of holding herself upright just slipped for a beat.

"Sure."

"No pineapple."

I blink. "On pizza?"

"On anything. I don't trust people who do that."

"Noted for the threat assessment."

"Mock me and I'll make you eat kale."

"That's terrorism."

"That's nutrition."

Once we've ordered, she asks if I want to watch a movie. My chest tightens—because she asked instead of pretending she didn't want company.

"A movie?" I say.

Lenni shrugs. "Or one of those mindless home-reno shows."

"I've seen those. They treat picking a backsplash like a moral victory."

"Exactly."

I sit on the far end of the couch, choosing the distance deliberately — not to avoid her, but because I've learned she needs space the way some people need oxygen.

She drops onto the opposite end, feet tucked beneath her, remote in hand, chin lifted in quiet defense. She tucks her feet under herself a second time, adjusting like she's searching for a position that doesn't ache.

Her gaze flicks briefly to the space between us — a quick assessment, almost imperceptible — like she expected it, or maybe like she's relieved I made the decision first.

Grits watches this silent negotiation from the rug. Then, like he's made an executive decision, he stands, stretches, and pads over to me.

He climbs up into my lap with that little dog confidence.

I blink down at him. "Buddy—"

Lenni's eyes soften – just for a second – before sharpening again, like she caught herself approving something she refuses to name.

"Oh my God."

Grits ignores her completely, settling like this is where he belongs.

I rest a hand on his back, slow and steady as he melts instantly.

Lenni's mouth tightens, the fight between amusement and resistance playing out across her face.

"Traitor," she mutters at him.

The room settles.

Her knee bounces.

Not restless — more like she's burning off the last of her adrenaline before exhaustion wins.

She catches me watching.

It stops.

"You're staring," she accuses.

"I'm observing."

"That's staring with benefits."

I grin.

"You're too mellow for a man who tackles strangers for a living," she mutters.

"I didn't tackle anybody."

"You intercepted. Like a football player with a conscience."

I lean back. "I take my job seriously. I don't take myself seriously."

She studies me, deciding if that's genuine or just another line. Quiet now: "Is that on purpose?"

"Yes."

"Why?"

I shrug. "Because panic is contagious. If I'm calm, everyone else gets permission to be."

Her throat moves; she looks away, annoyed by feeling something. "So you hand out permission slips?"

"Basically, I'm a guidance counselor."

She snorts. "God help us."

The room settles into a quiet rhythm until there's a knock on the door.

"I'll get it," I say, rising.

Lenni tilts her head. "Of course you will."

"You hired me."

"It wasn't my idea," she says. "They assigned you to me."

"Semantics."

We eat in silence until she says softly, "Thanks for coming." No drama, just her version of a confession. I let it stand.

"Of course," I reply. "You asked."

She hugs a throw pillow, voice sharper. "We leave again soon."

"I know."

"South," she adds. "South Carolina. Georgia. Miami."

"Yep."

She glances at me, like she wants to see if the itinerary means anything to me beyond logistics.

"There's supposed to be… a little beach break," she says, like she's pretending she doesn't care. "Two days."

"That's good," I tell her. "You need it."

Her eyes narrow. "There you go again – sounding like you know what I need."

"I've seen you run on adrenaline and stubbornness."

She opens her mouth to retort, then stops—because I said it as concern, as being on her side. She turns back to the screen, breathing steadier.

"Ever been to Miami?" she asks.

"Once," I say. "Work."

"Of course."

I shrug. "I saw the ocean from a parking garage."

She's incredulous. "Tragic."

"Efficient."

She grimaces. "You'll get sand in your boots and act like it's a personal affront."

"I'll get sand in my boots and continue doing my job."

"And stand there like a golden retriever with a gun, guarding me from seagulls and SPF."

I pause—she said golden retriever like she meant it. My grin softens. "Seagulls are aggressive."

Lenni rolls her eyes like she's annoyed at herself for starting this.

She rolls her eyes, mutters "Whatever," and turns back to the movie. But her shoulders loosen. Like the jokes did their job. Like the room finally feels more comfortable

Her legs stretch out, toes grazing my hip, dark

hair cascading over the cushion as her head sinks back.

Her weight settles heavier than before — not guarded now, just tired enough to forget she's supposed to stay upright.

Grits lifts his head at the shift. His ears twitch. He looks from me to Lenni like he's weighing his options.

Then—without ceremony—he crawls off my lap.

Not rushed. Not startled. Just... finished with me for now.

He moves straight into Lenni's space like he's done it a thousand times, nudging her forearm before curling against her ribs and circling until he finds the exact spot that makes her exhale.

He presses his warm little body into her, dropping his head heavy across her thigh.

Her fingers unfurl slowly, sinking into her fur.

A quiet sound leaves her—half sigh, half surrender—before she can stop it.

Without realizing, she shifts closer, the distance between us narrowing by inches.

I pretend not to notice.

Under the television's blue light, her breathing deepens. Eyelids flutter once, twice, then surrender to sleep. The fierce performer who commanded the stage hours ago now dozes with parted lips, her body curved subtly in my direction – not reaching, not asking, but no longer pulling away.

When the credits finish, I rise quietly, draping the throw blanket over her before returning to the far end of the couch.

I keep watch over her steady breathing, the locked door, the silence settling around us like something fragile worth protecting.

Morning light seeps through the blinds just as she stretches, her feet inadvertently landing in my lap.

Her lashes flutter against the morning light before recognition dawns. She jolts awake, tugging her legs back. "God, I hogged the whole couch," she says. "Did you get any sleep? You should've woke me up."

I offer a half-smile. "You weren't in my way. Wouldn't have dreamed of disturbing you."

Her eyes narrow like she's deciding whether to be touched or offended. "You're such a liar."

"Which part?"

"About the *dreamed* part." She rubs her face with both hands, as if she can wipe away having fallen asleep with her feet on me. "I drooled, didn't I?"

"You did not drool," I say immediately.

She squints. "That was too fast."

I raise a hand. "Okay, fine. There was... a *threat* of drool. Nothing actionable."

She laughs, then suppresses it, and it comes out breathy. Like she hates that I can still make her laugh in daylight.

I stand, stretch, and head to the kitchen, determined not to overthink that she woke up worrying about *me* sleeping instead of pretending she didn't care.

"I'm making coffee," I call.

"You don't even live here," she shoots back.

"I'm providing a service."

Lenni slides off the couch and follows barefoot with her hair tousled.

She stops in the doorway, watching me like I might do something wrong.

"What?" I ask, reaching for mugs.

"You look... domestic," she says like it's an insult. "It's unsettling."

"I contain multitudes," I reply – and grab a mug. I pour, then reach for the cream without asking.

Her brows lift. "Excuse me?"

I slide the mug across the counter. "Cream. No sugar."

She goes still for half a beat, like that landed somewhere it wasn't supposed to.

"You've been watching me," she says, accusation shaped like a question.

"I've been doing my job," I say easily, even as my mouth threatens to smile. "Tour bus doesn't exactly hide your routine."

She takes the cup anyway. One sip—and her eyes close briefly, just a flicker, like it hits a place in her that doesn't get touched often.

When she opens them again, they're sharper. Guard back up.

"Why are you being nice?" she asks, brow furrowed. "Like… actually nice. Not 'I'm doing my job' nice."

I'm trying not to say: *Because you looked smaller last night when your lungs wouldn't work, and it made something in me go feral.*

So I force a safe truth. "Because it helps. And because you let me."

A beat. She clears her throat, scoffing. "I didn't let you. I—"

"Asked," I finish quietly.

She opens her mouth to argue, shuts it, then mutters, "Don't make it a thing."

"I won't," I promise.

She stares at her coffee like it's suddenly complicated. "Good."

We stand in the quiet kitchen as the city wakes. The neon's gone. It feels almost normal.

Lenni sips again, sets the mug down, then hesitates at the counter's edge. Suddenly, she flicks my shirt at the shoulder. "You're still looming."

I blink. "I am not."

"You are," she insists, already backing away toward the hall like she didn't just touch me on purpose. "Try harder, Hank."

"It's Harlan," I call after her.

Her grin is small and wicked. "Sure it is."

She disappears down the hall, and I'm left holding coffee with a new, quiet thought settling in my chest: she didn't sleep because the movie

was boring.
    She slept because I was there.
    And that changes the math.

CHAPTER 7

Lennon

South Carolina

On tour, you can find sleep if you look hard enough.

Daylight, though? That's the unicorn.

When we roll during actual sunlight hours, it feels like we've hacked the system.

When we roll during actual sunlight hours, it feels like we've hacked the system. The world outside isn't just headlights bouncing off highway signs — it's fields, rivers, sky stretching wide enough to breathe. Everyone moves around the bus like we've been granted temporary parole.

Just past the Nashville city limits, Ro slaps a deck of cards against her palm.

"Get over here," she announces, grin edged with mischief. "Daylight hours mean normal people activities, and I refuse to waste them."

Kai's steady tapping against the table slows the moment Hank steps into the space – not stopping entirely, just shifting rhythm, recalibrating. Her gaze flicks up once, quick and assessing, measuring threat level, energy, intention.

It's subtle enough that most people would miss it. I don't. Kai reads rooms the way other people read weather forecasts — quietly, instinctively, always preparing.

"Join us." Ro demands, already dealing cards.

"On duty," he replies automatically.

Ro narrows her eyes, unimpressed. "Mandatory team bonding."

His gaze flicks to mine — a silent question.

I lift one brow. "Refuse and she'll haunt you forever."

The corner of his mouth shifts, almost a smile.

"Sit," Ro says again, softer this time but no less absolute.

And he does.

Not with reluctance or surrender. Just a quiet decision – like stepping into a circle and understanding the rules without needing them explained.

For the next hour, I watch him thaw.

Not dramatically or obviously.

Piece by careful piece.

Ro needles him relentlessly, testing boundaries the way she does with anyone she's deciding whether to trust. Kai's rhythm steadies again, tapping returning to its earlier tempo now that she's logged him somewhere between *safe* and *unknown.* Sin watches without looking like she's watching at all — quiet judgment wrapped in stillness.

And Hank lets it happen.

He doesn't dominate the space.

Doesn't withdraw from it.

Just.. exists inside it.

Which, for us, is the real test.

Somewhere between Ro accusing him of "hovering over his cards like a federal agent" and Sin demolishing his hand with surgical precision, I realize something I wasn't expecting.

He's not trying to win.

He's learning us.

We reach for the same card simultaneously – Hank's fingertips graze mine, a fleeting contact that sends electricity up my arm.

My heartbeat trips over itself. I cover it with a smirk. Like I'm not a person with a pulse.

His gaze snaps to mine, pupils dilating slightly.

Ro's eyes narrow, filing it away for later.

Grits chooses that moment to wedge himself between us.

Hank drops a hand to scratch behind his ears — slow, familiar now — like this isn't new anymore, like my dog trusting him isn't quietly rearranging something inside me.

I don't pull back when his shoulder brushes mine this time. A week ago I would have shifted away automatically. Now my body just... stays.

His knuckles graze my thigh.

Barely.

Not intentional.

But my body reacts anyway.

I don't move.

Neither does he.

His hand pauses just a fraction before continuing — controlled, deliberate — like he felt it too and chose not to acknowledge it.

The warmth lingers longer than it should, and instead of tensing, my muscles loosen — betraying me in ways I'm not ready to examine.

Later, after I win a hand, he nudges my shoulder with casual ease.

I retaliate by brushing his wrist when he scowls at his cards.

Small touches.

Accumulating.

Harmless on the surface.

Dangerous underneath.

Each one leaving a quiet hum beneath my skin.

Somewhere between the first hand and now, I've stopped tracking the space between us — stopped measuring distance like it's survival.

And every time it happens, I remind myself:

Don't confuse protection with chemistry.

Crossing into South Carolina, our tour bus shifts into something softer – guitars strumming from the bunks, laughter threading through conversations.

Hank's settled into the rhythm too — dry humor slipping through his stoic exterior just enough to make Ro grin like she's discovered buried treasure.

Not relaxed.

Just… integrated.

And without noticing when it started, I lean

back into the seat knowing exactly where he is without looking — like my body keeps count for me now.

And for once, I exhale.

Until South Carolina greets us with Colby Bridges.

He materializes at the bus steps before I've fully descended. Sunshine-bright smile already deployed.

"Vale! Been waiting for you."

His hand lands on my lower back.

I slide forward smoothly, leaving it behind.

"Tracking arrivals now?"

"Just yours."

Ro watches with open amusement.

Hank doesn't intervene – just exists nearby, steady enough that the air changes.

Colby clocks him instantly. His smile tightens at the edges.

"Packed schedule today?"

"Completely," I say, already walking. "Rehearsal, press, sound check."

He falls into step beside me, orbiting too close. "I can help you get ready."

"I'm good," I say with sugary finesse – sweet voice, sharp spine.

He laughs like I've flirted. I haven't.

All day, he persists.

A hand at my shoulder as he passes. A lean-in that steals half my space when he talks. A familiarity he wears like a jacket — easy, practiced, deliberate.

I counter with professional deflections that sound polite enough to pass as cooperation:

"Tight timeline."

"Production meeting."

"Vocal rest."

Each one delivered with a smile sharp enough to cut through steel if he bothered to notice.

And when he doesn't take the hint, I take the space.

It's hellfire hot.

Sweat glues leather to my thighs, and the spotlights burn against my skin like a fever.

Three thousand voices crash together – a wall of sound thick enough to press against my ribs. Beer. Salt. Electricity.

I hit the stage and muscle memory takes over.

I transform.

I snarl lyrics, bare teeth, throw my voice to the rafters without hesitation. I become untouchable, unbreakable, unflinching.

Yet through it all, I feel his eyes.

Hank.

At the edge of the stage.

Scanning sightlines.

Watching exits.

Guarding perimeters.

Guarding me.

The final chorus breaks and the audience erupts like thunder. I let it crash over me, hoping it might rinse away everything complicated.

Backstage, I'm barely toweled off when Ro and Colby descend.

"We're celebrating," Ro declares, already buzzing with energy.

Colby edges closer. "Georgia's just down the road. One late night won't kill us."

I drag a towel across my neck, keeping my tone casual. "Pass."

Ro clutches invisible pearls. "The real Lenni must be tied up somewhere."

"Just exhausted and drenched," I say, like admitting weakness is a liability, like if I say it lightly nobody can weaponize it later.

Colby's fingers circle my arm.

"Just one round."

I step forward smoothly, letting his hand fall away without confrontation.

I slip away, frictionless. "It's still a no."

Ro's eyebrow lifts. "This wouldn't have anything to do with—"

"This has to do with feeling like a swamp," I interrupt, forcing humor into my voice. "Every joint aches."

Without waiting for their next attempt, I move toward the exit.

Hank appears at my side without a word.

He doesn't ask questions. Doesn't crowd me.

We've still got back-to-back shows ahead and miles of asphalt between them.

I squeeze into what passes for a shower on this bus—a glorified Tupperware container with a drain. Tepid water dribbles over my skin while the generators vibration travels up through my heels.

Whatever.

Good enough to wash away the sweat and smoke and strangers' perfume.

My bed in my little private room waits like a coffin with clean sheets. I climb in, headphones clamped over my ears, and burrow under the blankets with Grits.

"Everlong" by Foo Fighters drowns out my thoughts while I thumb through social media, feeling my consciousness start to fray at the edges.

Then my bladder announces itself—because of course it does.

With a groan, I untangle myself, headphones still blasting. Irritated and half-conscious I shuffle down the little hall.

The bathroom door is closed. Light glows beneath it.

I don't think.

I open it.

And freeze.

Steam rushes at me, hot and thick as breath.

Hank stands beneath the spray, back turned, muscles carved into his shoulders, water cascading down the hollow of his spine.

He whips around at the sound.

Our eyes collide.

Time shatters.

He doesn't move — not embarrassed, not angry — just caught in the same gravity that's pinning me to the floor.

Water slices over him, defining every ridge of muscle, every jagged scar I've never dared to imagine this close.

The air between us ignites – raw, dangerous.

His jaw clenches hard enough I can see the pulse hammering in his throat.

My lungs forget how to work.

Something explodes between us – hunger, need, something we've been drowning since the moment we met.

He reaches for a towel without breaking the connection burning between us.

Reality crashes back like a slap.

"Oh— shit — sorry—" I slam the door so hard it shudders in its frame

Heart thundering.

Skin on fire.

Inside my room, I collapse against the wall, gulping air.

Not because I saw him naked.

Because of how he devoured me with that look.

Not startled.

Just... starving.

And now there's no hiding from this inferno between us anymore.

CHAPTER 8

Harlan

Florida

Georgia clears the sweep – no corridor breaches, no stray hands, no hidden surprises in the crowd.

Just heat, bright rigs, booming speakers – Lenni at the top of her game, and me doing mine: locking down every exit before anything can slip through. Routine is the only prayer I trust.

We handle the long haul south with Lenni curling over her notebook between hands, pen tapping her lip as if the song is knocking from inside her skull.

I only join when she snaps, "Sit. If you're gonna glare, at least pull your weight."

"I don't glare."

"You hover aggressively," she shoots back.

I sit.

Their idea of "relaxing" involves shouting, cheating accusations and ruthless competition. Behind Lenni's sweet smile lurks something razor-sharp.

Her fingers brush mine as she deals a card. Then she flicks my arm when I take the pot.

Small contacts. Accidental enough to ignore. Intentional enough not to be.

My pulse jumps anyway. I catch her breath hitch once.

Reflex.

Truth slipping through muscle memory.

We don't mention the shower.

We also don't pretend it didn't happen.

The silence around it has weight now – not avoidance, but awareness.

When she passes me in the hallway, her shoulder grazes mine. Eyes forward. Body steady.

Like nothing changed.

Like everything did.

Boundaries built my security career.

Client relationships: strictly professional.

Distance maintained. Fraternization prohibited. Rules carved into bone.

They're also the only reason I can stand five feet from her without losing control.

By the time we pull into Miami, salt air sits heavy on my tongue.

The condo is swept, the route's clean, the schedule tight.

Everything should feel contained.

It doesn't.

Lenni is too quiet, like pressure building behind glass.

And I go quiet too. Because if I break the silence, I might say something that ruins us both.

The show is pure fire.

Miami roared louder than Georgia—hotter, brighter, hungrier.

She closes the set like she owned the city. She stepped forward, mic in hand, her grin sharpened into a weapon.

"Miami," she purred, dragging the word out like trouble. "Y'all have been loud as hell tonight."

The crowd lost their minds. Two taps to her chest—habit, ritual—and the front row mirrored her move, like she'd taught them how to breathe. Then she pointed the mic at them and let them scream themselves hoarse.

Clean exit. Tight formation. Straight to freedom.

I was already mapping the corridor—staff badges, doorways, lingering bodies—my attention tracked everything automatically, cataloging patterns, searching for anything that broke from expected movement.

That's when it hit.

Sin's gaze flicks toward him before he even speaks – tracking threat before anyone else registers it.

"Lennon Vale!"

That drawl carried through the noise before I even turned. Too familiar. Too confident.

Colby Bridges.

He appeared the moment she slipped behind the curtain, stepping into her space as if it belonged to him, as if access had already been granted something outside of her control.

Sweat-dark curls peeked from beneath his hat,

his grin tilted just enough to suggest the night revolved around him and she was simply another highlight in it.

"Hell of a set," he said, leaning in too close.

Lenni answered with a practiced "thanks," the kind she could deliver without thinking, and immediately began weaving through the crew, creating distance on autopilot. He fell into step beside her anyway, matching her stride with easy persistence.

Like he'd learned women rarely make scenes if you keep things framed as friendly.

"Both bands are going out tonight," he announced. "It's Miami!"

I adjusted my stance without drawing attention—relaxed shoulders, neutral posture, body angled to close distance if needed while maintaining the illusion of space.

Lenni mustered a smile, but it wasn't for me or her team. It was the one reserved for rooms where refusal contained consequences.

"Sounds fun," she said lightly, because flat-out refusal would be a headline before reached the elevator. Because someone – Evie – would call that headline "avoidable."

His grin sharpened.

"Good," he said. "Because you're coming."

My jaw tightened.

I should have been indifferent. Men like Colby orbited principals like Lenni constantly—loud, charming, opportunistic, convinced proximity meant invitation.

Except I'm not indifferent.

I saw her shoulders stiffen beneath leather. The way she angled away without breaking stride. The half-smile that didn't reach her eyes. The subtle flex of her hand at her side like she wanted to shove him but chose professionalism instead.

And I remembered the bus.

The way her eyes had looked when she caught me in the shower. The way mine held hers because neither of us knew how to retreat without acknowledging what existed between us.

Chemistry didn't guarantee consent.

But it made the wrong men believe it did.

He kept talking, hovering, filling the air between them with easy charm designed to look harmless.

Lenni kept walking.

And I kept pace—silent, steady, doing my job.

But underneath protocol and contract, one through rose sharp and undeniable:

If she asks me to cut him off, I will.

And I don't be gentle about it.

The driver drops us at the club entrance like

cargo being delivered late.

Pure Miami.

Bass thuds hard enough to rattle ribs. Neon light spilling across palm trunks and pavement, turning everything electric and slightly unreal. Sticky heat loosens boundaries the way alcohol does, and that alone makes the environment a risk.

Inside, the DJ blasts old hits—Pitbull's *Hotel Room Service* pulsing through speakers loud enough to erase conversation. The lighting stays low, the crowd packed tight, bodies moving with abandon. Half the room looks like they've forgotten clothes exist. The air smells like expensive cologne, sweat, and something sharp enough to sting the back of my throat.

I keep my distance from Lenni—close enough to intercept, far enough that she never feels managed.

That's how it works with her.

Crowd her, and she bites.

Cage her, and everything burns.

Give her space, and she chooses her own exits.

We push through bodies toward the VIP section where Hollow Mesa waits, exactly as advertised: worn denim, scuffed boots, cocksure swagger worn like armor that never comes off.

Colby claims the head of the table like a throne, Stetson low, smile calibrated to pull attention.

He breathes it.

Craves it.

His bassist, Grady Fisher, lingers back with a tumbler already half-empty, while drummer Clint Baker anchors the group with linebacker shoulders and an easy laugh that never loses awareness of the room.

Clint's wife sits beside him, watchful and grounded in a way that felt quietly stabilizing.

I catalog everything—crowd density, blind spots, exits, behavioral patterns, who drinks too fast, who watches too hard.

Ro shatters routine instantly, sliding into the seat beside Hollow's guitarist, Blaize Crawford, like she's staking a claim.

He leans in, drawn by her chaos, trying to determine whether she's flirting or circling prey.

Her smile turns just slightly dangerous.

Which means she was either playing or protecting.

Lenni remains standing.

Calculating.

Positioned at the booth's edge where she can leave without obstruction, back angled toward open space instead of a wall. I stay visible but nonintrusive, close enough that she can reach me without feeling watched.

Before she even glances at a menu, Colby presses a drink into her hand.

I watch her fingers close around the glass. She doesn't drink. She holds it because refusing creates friction she doesn't have the energy for.

He leans in, mouth near her ear.

"You were so sexy up there, Len."

Her smile stays polite. Controlled. Professional.

Then she shifts—barely an inch—toward me.

Most wouldn't notice.

I do.

A quiet drift toward the nearest exit. Toward stability. Toward me.

"Appreciate it," she says lightly.

Colby's gaze flicks past her shoulder toward me – measuring, not curious.

"And that guard dog of yours? He always gotta hover?"

Lenni laughs once, sharp and contained.

"Hank's doing his job."

He makes a dismissive sound.

"He should relax," he says. "You're with friends."

Friends.

Sure.

I keep my posture neutral, refusing to step closer and give him the satisfaction of knowing he's provoked me. Still, my feet angle slightly inward—one inch, then another – not enough to challenge, just enough to intercept.

He leans in again, voice low.

"You ever wonder what it'd be like to break free and be with someone who doesn't treat you like glass for a night?"

Lenni goes still.

Not fear, control.

She tilts her head, lashes lowering, smile slow and deceptively sweet.

"Do you ever wonder," she says softly, voice edged like a blade, "what it'd be like to shut the fuck up once in a while?"

Colby laughs, loud and careless, completely missing the shift in the room.

Heads turn. Silence tightens.

She'd skins him cleanly without raising her voice.

Lenni lifts her drink and takes a slow sip, already done with him.

And I didn't move.

Because she doesn't need me to.

Ro's smile disappears entirely – humor gone, eyes sharp.

She slides in and tugs Lenni toward the bathroom, breezy and casual. I follow at a respectful distance, watching Colby recalibrate.

When Lenni returns, Ro resumes her seat like nothing had happened.

Colby finds her again anyway, sliding an arm around her waist.

Lenni goes stone still—not helpless, just calculating whether a scene is worth the fallout.

"I thought you bailed," he says.

"I don't bail," she replies coolly.

He drinks more, leaning closer.

"I'm telling you," he murmurs near her ear, "you and me? That'd be one hell of a story."

That's enough.

I step in—not aggressive, just present—placing myself between them like a door quietly closing, the movement so natural it barely registers as a decision.

"Ready to head out?" I ask her.

Colby scoffs.

"What, the bouncer calling last call?"

"I'm not a bouncer," I say evenly.

He laughs too loud. "Professional jealousy, then?"

I allow a micro-smirk. I've heard sharper digs from men who mattered more.

I don't look at him again.

Only her.

"Your car's outside," I tell her quietly. "If you want it."

An out. Clean. A rescue she never asked for—but one she clearly needs.

"Yeah," she says smoothly. "I want it."

Colby's grin falters. "Seriously?"

Lenni's eyes go cold.

"Seriously."

Then she meets my gaze.

"Lead the way, Hank."

That nickname strikes me—like a leash she pretends not to hold. Like she's daring me to read it as intimacy instead of instruction.

"Copy that."

We step out into the Miami night, bass still thrumming behind us, and I log two truths:

Colby Bridges keeps pushing until someone stops him.

And Lenni Vale never asks me to save her – but she takes my exit anyway.

And the real problem isn't just Colby.

It's that when she's cornered, her body turns toward me like it already knows where relief lives.

And mine answers every time.

CHAPTER 9

Lennon

Florida

The morning light slices through the gap in the drapes, cutting across the room in a thin blade of gold.

I stay motionless on the mattress anyway, thumbs moving over my phone screen while I pretend my stomach isn't tightening with every notification that appears.

I already know what I'm going to find.

Still, I scroll.

And there it is.

The footage is grainy but unmistakable—already viral. Last night at the bar: me pressed against the wall, Colby invading my space, his head dipped toward mine like we're sharing secrets instead of negotiating boundaries.

The camera angle is merciless. My profile turned away, his mouth near my ear, our silhouettes frozen in what looks like intimacy.

Paused just long enough to lie convincingly.

> "LENNI VALE SETS TOUR ON FIRE
> WITH HOLLOW MESA'S BAD BOY"

Quick. Ridiculous. Predictable.
And still – it stings.

Not because it hurts.

Because it's familiar.

Because it works.

The clip doesn't capture my rigid shoulders, or the untouched cocktail I abandoned, or the slow crawl of revulsion up my spine when he stepped too close.

It doesn't show the way I shifted toward the only safe exit in the room

I close the tab before the comments load.

Movement is the only thing that burns this feeling out of my system – the sensation of being turned into a story that doesn't belong to me.

I open messages.

Me: *Need the gym. Now.*
Hank: *On it. Outside in 120 seconds..*

Of course he is.

I pull on black high-waisted leggings and a sports bra, twisting my hair into a messy knot as adrenaline replaces sleep.

Hank is already in the hallway when I step out.

Calm and steady in a way that makes me want to shove him just to see if he wobbles.

His gaze flicks over me once – quick, controlled – then returns to my face like he's resetting himself.

Always professional.

I hate that my eyes do the opposite.

Broad shoulders under a plain tee. Strong forearms. The quiet authority in his posture that says the world can throw whatever it wants and he won't budge.

A man built to stand between things.

"Morning, Hank," I say, too casual.

"It's Harlan," he replies automatically.

"Sure, it is."

A corner of his mouth moves.

"Gym?"

"Gym." I confirm. "If I don't move my body, I'm gonna start a fight with an alligator."

"I'd pay to see that," he says, voice dry.

"No you wouldn't."

"You're probably right," he admits easily. "Too much paperwork."

Every time I bare teeth, he refuses to flinch.

And that unsettles me more than resistance ever did.

We're halfway down the corridor when a door carefully opens, like someone's trying not to be noticed.

Rowan Kelly slips out, hair wild, wearing a hoodie that definitely isn't hers.

She freezes the moment she sees us, eyes widening just enough to betray guilt before she schools her expression into innocence.

I stop too, one eyebrow lifting slowly.

"Ro?" I draw the word out, already suspicious.

"Don't," she says immediately, pointing at me like she knows exactly where this is going.

"Oh, I haven't even started." I reply, shifting

my weight as amusement curls under my irritation.

Her gaze flick to Hank, assessing him with that sharp, mischievous curiosity she reserves for new variables.

"Morning, Officer."

"I'm not a cop," he replies flatly, like he's reciting a mantra he's said too many times already.

Ro's grin widens. "Sure, Hank."

I cough to hide a laugh, because if I actually let it out, I'll have to admit she's funny – and I'm not ready for that level of emotional vulnerability before coffee.

She slides past us, key already in hand, then pauses at the door and leans closer, stage-whispering like she's narrating a scandal.

"Have fun working out. Try not to hurt him."

I flip her off without hesitation.

She salutes dramatically and disappears inside, the door clicking shut behind her.

Silence settles or half a beat.

Hank clears his throat. "So.. that happened."

"We're not gonna talk about it."

"Copy."

We start walking again without discussing it, falling to step automatically – not close enough to touch, but closer than strangers would walk. I hate that my shoulders loosen anyway.

Because Rowan is chaos.

And chaos, sometimes, feels like relief.

The lobby is hushed in that curated luxury

way — muted lamps, gleaming floors, everything polished to perfection. The receptionist looks up with a professional smile that brightens noticeably when she sees Hank approaching.

Then her eyes land to me.

Recognition flashes.

"Ms. Vale," she whispers.

Hank steps forward smoothly, posture relaxed but authoritative. "We'd like the gym to ourselves for the next hour."

She blinks. "Um—"

"Security detail," he adds quickly.

Color drains from her face as she nods quickly, already reaching for the phone.

"Of course. Absolutely."

I shift slightly closer without thinking, positioning myself at his shoulder rather than behind him — like I'm aligning with him instead of being shielded by him.

She slides a fob across the counter. "I'll lock the doors. No one enters without your okay."

"Thank you," Hank says politely.

Her smile lingers on him too long.

Something sharp tightens in my chest.

"Let me know if there's anything else I can do for you, Mr.—"

"Harlan," he cuts in, clipped. "Just Harlan."

Her eyes brighten.

I clear my throat louder than necessary.

"We're good," I say quickly, already turning away.

It's not jealousy.

That's what I tell myself as we move toward the hallway together.

Hank falls into step beside me, quiet for a few beats. Then, without looking directly at me, he says softly:

"You don't have to pretend you're unaffected for me."

I blink. "I'm not pretending anything."

His mouth curves faintly, not arguing, not pushing.

And then he moves ahead to sweep the doorway like he didn't just rearrange something inside my chest.

When he nods, I step inside.

Mirrors line one wall, bright lights reflecting movement from every angle. The smell of sanitizer hangs sharp in the air.

My eyes dart to the mirrors, then to him, then away—being seen without being consumed is… unsettling.

Especially after realizing exactly how much both of us notice when we pretend not to.

"We're seriously doing this?" I ask.

"Doing what?"

"Pretending you're not overanalyzing me in spandex."

He blinks once, then his mouth quirks as if he's fighting a smile.

"Lenni," he breathes, "I am a master at compartmentalizing."

"Liar."

"All right," he admits, still light. "Some thoughts are... too enthusiastic."

A pause.

His gaze flicks—quick, controlled—then snaps back to my face.

"Professionally," he adds.

I let out a sharp laugh despite myself, and roll my shoulders like I can physically shake the moment loose – remind both of us to cool it.

"You work out a lot?" I ask offhand.

He arches an eyebrow. "My physique isn't convincing?"

"Ohhh," I tease. "So modest."

He considers. "I'm somewhere between 'gym rat' and 'capable of hoisting you over my shoulder if needed.'"

My brain betrays me instantly with an image I absolutely did not request, so I pivot toward the squat rack like it's a lifeboat.

I load the bar, plant my feet, brace my core, and drop into a squat.

I don't look at him, but I feel him watching.

I rise, reset, and drop again – deeper this time – focusing on the burn in my legs instead of the awareness prickling across my skin.

He steps closer.

"Your knee is drifting," he tells me quietly.

"It's not." I reply, pushing up through the rep.

"It is." He says, just as calm, just as certain.

I rack the bar harder than necessary, then turn

toward him with narrowed eyes.

"Are you coaching me now?"

"I'm protecting your joints," he replies serenely, completely unbothered by my edge.

Our eyes lock in the mirror – his gaze anchored on me, not intrusive but impossible to ignore. Then he murmurs, softer, careful: "May I?"

The politeness shocks me more than the correction ever could. My jaw clenches, and something inside me uncoils.

"Don't make it weird." I warn.

"Understood."

He closes the gap with deliberate slowness. His fingertips brush the outside of my knee—barely a whisper of contact, yet it ignites a slow burn through my leg.

"Push out," he breathes, husky and intimate. "Track over the foot." I obey, my movement suddenly precise, powerful.

I rise.

"Better," he says, low praise vibrating between us.

In the mirror, our eyes meet again—heat wrapped in restraint, desire tangled with professionalism—the tension of standing inches from a flame without letting yourself get burned. I rack the bar and step back, heart pounding.

"If you flex one more time while coaching," I say dryly, forcing humor back into my voice, "you're going to breach your contract."

He grins, unabashed. "Noted."

I feign irritation and head for the bench.

"Spot me?" I call over my shoulder, the words casual but laced with intent.

He's behind me before I finish the set, calloused hands hovering under the bar—close enough to intervene, distant enough to let me own the lift. My skin prickles at his nearness: the heat of his body, the cedar scent of his soap, the hard promise pressing just above my forehead.

The last rep trembles between us. I quake with fatigue. He leans in, guiding the bar back onto the rack. His fingertips graze mine—electric, louder than the metallic clang of iron settling.

Silence thickens the air, charged and dangerous.

"The tabloids are going to be brutal today," I murmur, sitting up, chest heaving.

"About you and Colby," he states, steady, not quite a question.

I stare at my chalked hands as if the dust will anchor me from falling apart. Looking at him now would be too much.

His voice remains calm, infuriatingly so. "Would you rather I distract you from it," he asks quietly, "or talk you through it?"

Something twists in my chest at how badly I want to whisper—

Can't we do both?

Not in a warm, indulgent way — in the curated, calculated way of somewhere designed to photograph well. White tablecloths glow under soft lighting. Candles burn inside glass cylinders that distort the flame just enough to feel intentional. A server welcomes us with a smile that feels rehearsed, like we're part of the performance instead of guests.

We claim a long table in the back. My people: handlers turned human.

Ro slumps into her seat immediately, limbs loose, already bored. Kai settles beside her with quiet precision. Sin takes the end position with her back to the wall.

Harper hovers over her phone, half-working, half-listening.

Mila chooses a seat close enough to hear everything and far enough to pretend she isn't.

Evie arrives last – polished, lethal.

She slides into her chair like gravity bends around her, like this entire environment exists for her convenience.

Hank doesn't fully join us.

He takes a seat a few feet away — close enough to observe, distant enough to maintain his line between professional and personal.

He doesn't insert himself into the conversation. He simply exists within it — a quiet perimeter.

It should make me feel watched.

Instead, it makes my lungs remember how to behave.

First ten minutes feel almost normal.

As normal as my life ever is.

Ro stealing an olive off someone else's plate, Kai quietly sliding a candle away from Harper's sleeve before it becomes a fire hazard. Sin tracking movement in the room like a silent metronome.

Then Evie taps her phone.

"That clip's trending again," she says lightly. "Morning push is live – picked up by three accounts already."

Ro groans. "Oh God."

Evie smiles wider.

"This is good."

"Absolutely not," I mutter.

"It is," she corrects smoothly. "Engagement's up."

"Except I didn't consent."

Evie tilts her head like I've said something charmingly naïve.

"You performed," she says. "You're being emotional."

"I'm being accurate," I shoot back. "It's not true."

"And that," she says, voice soft but final, "does

not matter."

Her eyes don't blink when she says it, like the truth is optional.

Ro looks ready to cause damage with a butter knife.

Mila cuts in quietly. "Evie."

Evie lifts one hand in patient dismissal, as though we're the ones escalating.

"Lenni, you've worked so hard. Don't stall your own momentum. This is an opportunity."

She says opportunity the way someone says inevitability — soft enough to feel supportive, firm enough to remove choice.

I stare at her.

"You want me to... what? Smile harder?"

"Exactly," she beams. "Keep doing what you're doing."

Like she didn't just admit she's steering it.

"What I'm doing," I say flatly, "is trying not to commit a felony in public."

Ro snorts.

Harper chokes on laughter.

Even Mila's mouth twitches.

Evie remains unbothered. "Here's the thing— Texas."

My stomach drops. "No."

She keeps going like I didn't speak.

"Dallas show. Big market. We're adding a duet."

The table shifts subtly – chairs angling toward me like a silent formation.

Kai's stops tagging – the silence louder than anger. Sun doesn't speak, but her fork pauses midair like she's deciding how much violence is socially acceptable.

Ro's grin sharpens into something feral.

"Oh, she's serious."

Evie nods.

"Colby and Lenni. One song, two stars. It amplifies the narrative, fuels engagement, gives fan a moment." Her smile brightens. "And keeps you in control."

My fork hits the plate with a sharp clink.

"You did not clear that with me."

"We don't have to clear everything with you." The words land sweet, warm enough to pretend it's care: "That's why you have a team."

Ro's chair scrapes back.

Mila's voice slices the air again: "Evie."

For a fraction of a second, Evie's composure flickers under Mila's stare.

Then she resets.

"Dallas is happening," she says, voice velvet-soft but razor-edged. "You can ride the flames – or become ash."

"Use me," I spit back, barely audible.

Evie tilts her head, predatory. "Lenni, you're a brand."

Artic water floods down my veins, freezing everything it touches.

Ro lunges forward, voice dripping honey-venom. "Evie, babe, call her just a brand one more time and I'll create a headline that'll incinerate your career."

Evie dismisses her with a flick of manicured fingers.

"You're all so protective. It's adorable."

Her eyes drill into mine, unblinking."

I'm the crowbar she'll use to pry open millions.

My jaw locks. I should scream. I should overturn this table.

But the future unfolds with brutal clarity – emails marked urgent, contracts with highlighted signature lines, conversations masquerading as partnership.

The trap is elegant.

Fight, and I'm a nightmare

Surrender, and I'm a team player.

"So what?" My voice cracks. "I writhe onstage with a man who makes my skin crawl?"

"It doesn't have to be explicit," Evie counters, voice slick as oil. "Just one electric look. Let their imaginations catch fire.

Her phone clicks beneath her blood-red nails.

"A lingering touch. A whispered word. They'll build their fantasies."

Ro retches dramatically.

Kai's eyes flash to mine. "Lenni..."

"I'm fine," I lie through clenched teeth.

Evie keeps talking — timelines, PR angles, song options.

The syllables crash into white noise as blood pounds in my temples. The walls constrict, and desperate, I find Hank.

He sits apart. Legs planted wide, forearms commanding the chair like territory.

Vigilant.

Not watching – but when our eyes collide, his entire being locks onto me.

No demands. No judgement. Just fortress-solid presence. A silent promise that needs no voice: *Say the word and I end this*.

My throat constricts. The answer claw inside me – yes.

I swallow it down.

I hold his gaze until my racing pulse steadies, my backbone reinforces, my body remembers its sovereignty.

Mine.

Even when they auction it like merchandise.

I turn back to Evie and raise my chin, the titanium smile sliding into place – the armor I wear in battle rooms like this.

Under the table, my nails draw blood from my palm.

Because what terrifies me isn't headlines.

It's that when voices rise to drown me – my soul reaches blindly.

For him.

The meeting breaks in a scatter of chairs and voices, tension snapping but not disappearing.

I stand too fast. The room tilts just slightly — enough that I feel it.

Hank is beside me before I register him moving.

Not crowding. Not claiming.

Just there.

His hand settles at my waist — warm, steady, grounding.

Not pulling me. Not guiding me.

Holding.

The contact is light enough I could step away, but firm enough that my body recognizes safety before my mind catches up.

We walk toward the door together, the others moving ahead, voices fading into background noise.

His thumb shifts once — barely there — a quiet check-in rather than a demand.

"You good?" he murmurs, low enough only I hear.

The question isn't pressure. It's permission.

I exhale slowly.

"Working on it," I admit.

His arm doesn't tighten. He doesn't pull me closer.

He just stays.

And somehow that steadiness feels louder than anything said in the room behind us.

CHAPTER 10

HARLAN

Florida

Miami was meant to be a reset.
And under the Florida sun, it nearly was.
For twelve hours, nothing hunted us.
No cameras. No crowds. No shadows trying to slip past security lines.
Just quiet.
Quiet is dangerous when you don't remember how to live inside it.
Lenni crashed. Hard. The kind of unconscious, unreachable slumber that only comes after weeks of running on nothing but willpower and Red Bull.
I maintained my post outside her suite during her massage—stance wide, gaze alert, acting like I couldn't pinpoint her exact location from the deep sigh that drifted through the door crack.
The sound shouldn't register.
It does anyway.
Not desire — not that.
Something closer to relief.

Like proof she finally let go of the wheel.
My phone buzzed somewhere between the masseuse's arrival and my second security

sweep.

I stayed rooted, but my chest tightened anyway – because there are only two people who usually call.

"Hey," I said, softening the word without meaning to.

My mother didn't waste time. "I saw you on TV."

Fantastic.

"That wasn't me," I muttered, even though my mouth was already pulling into a smile.

"Oh please," my sister chimed in—chipper, intrusive, unreasonably alert. "We saw you do your human shield move. All brooding and heroic. Mom's already planning your funeral after you take a bullet for Miss Famous."

"Everything's fine," I replied mechanically, eyes tracking a housekeeping cart drifting down the hall. But my voice wasn't mechanical anymore. It never was with them.

Mom's skeptical grunt spoke volumes. "Getting enough to eat?"

"Yes."

"Sleep?"

"Enough."

"And are you being smart," my sister added, "or are you being… heroic?"

I almost laughed. "Both."

"That's not what I asked," my sister sang. "Hero is the guy who thinks he can carry the whole world in one fist."

I kept scanning the corridor, voice neutral. "This is just the job."

"Always is," Mom said softly, and the softness lands like a bruise. "You've been saying that since you were fifteen."

My grip tightened on the phone. Dad died when we were kids—too young, too sudden—and I filled the spaces he left like it was my responsibility.

No one asked me to.

That never stopped me.

Mom's voice dipped. "Harlan… it's hard when you're gone."

My throat worked once. "I know," I said, quieter. "I hate that it's hard."

My sister tried to keep it light. "Mom's been hovering by her phone like it's a life support machine. It's annoying. Tell her to stop."

"Don't talk about your mother like that," Mom snapped automatically, then sighed. "Your sister's right."

I almost smiled again. They were a mess without me and furious about it, which was… familiar. "I'll call more," I said. A promise, not a dodge.

My sister made an offended noise.

"False. You text like a WWII telegram. Two words and a period."

"I'm busy," I said, and immediately softened it—"but I'll do better."

Mom's voice gentled. "You don't have to prove anything to us."

That one hit. Because I'd been proving things since Dad died.

"I'm not," I said, even if it wasn't entirely true. "I'm just… working."

A pause.

Then Mom, very quiet: "We're proud of you. We're just still trying to get used to you being gone."

My gaze flicked to Lenni's door again, then back down the empty hallway. The job wants me hard. My family wants me human.

"I'll call later," I said. "After we move."

"Alright," Mom whispered. "Call later."

My sister had to be last. "Pull any heroics and I'll hunt you down."

"Understood," I said, and this time I actually laughed—low and real. "Love you."

"Love you," they echoed—two voices overlapping.

I ended the call, slid my phone back into my pocket, and reset my stance like nothing inside me had shifted. Like I wasn't suddenly aware of the distance in miles and years.

Because this job didn't pause for family check-ins. And Lenni didn't get reprieve unless I held the line. Her peace depended on my constant vigilance.

But my mother and sister depended on me too. They had for a long time. And being away didn't stop that—it just made it ache.

I kept watch through the manicures, through

what should have been a simple meal but became a celebration with her bandmates, through genuine laughter, untainted by flashbulbs or recording phones.

For the first time since I'd signed the contract, we glimpsed something like tranquility.

And the only thing that felt dangerous wasn't the crowd. It was how much I wanted to stay in two places at once.

But tonight the armor goes back on – hers first, then mine.

One more nightclub. One more elevated section roped off from the masses. One more space crammed with sweaty bodies, thundering beats, and men who believe their attention should be treated as payment.

One more evening where Lennon Vale transforms into what they expect—all swagger, fire, and sharp edges—because at some point, social media decided it owned a piece of her, performance or not.

Ownership without permission. Access without consequence.

That transformation? I despised it.

Yet I recognized its necessity.

And therein lay my conflict.

Miami's heat slaps against me—wet and heavy, the city itself breathing. The security detail fans out behind the band, checking radios, scanning everything: sidewalks, tinted car windows, lingerers.

Lenni's holding my bicep, black dress speaking volumes—not an ounce of softness in its sleek lines. A garment built for battle. She wears her dark hair loose tonight, cascading over one shoulder. Every detail intentional. Every choice armor.

She doesn't acknowledge me as I open the car door.

She never needs to.

I hold it open regardless.

"Your chariot awaits," I say, cursing my inability to maintain professional distance.

The corner of her mouth quirks upward. "Behave yourself."

"Just doing my job," I reply, casual.

She enters the vehicle with the confidence of someone who commands every molecule around her.

Exiting, she moves with practiced efficiency—a rhythm born from necessity: keep moving, stay unpredictable, leave no opening.

My palm finds the small of her back instinctively, before I can think better of it.

I mean to guide her forward — but my hand stays a fraction too long, steadying instead of steering.

A fleeting touch, automatic and dangerously familiar, certainly beyond the scope of my employment agreement.

She doesn't lean into it.

She doesn't flinch either.

And for one quiet second, neither of us breaks the contact.

That might be worse.

As if she's deciding what my hand means. As if meaning is something she controls.

We slip in through a side door, flanked by two venue staff and one of our guys scouting ahead. I recognize *Tipsy* by J-Kwon thumping through the walls—as if the DJ is weaponizing nostalgia—and strobes sliced color across the corridor.

This place sells bottled fantasies and calls it freedom.

In the VIP corridor the air is cooler, quieter in that exclusive way.

The suite Hollow Mesa booked is already heaving. Crew members, managers, PR reps, and a few loose faces from Hollow Mesa milled about.

Evie hovers, phone in hand, smile polished, eyes calculating every angle.

I survey the exits, tally bodies, note the mirrors, the bartender, and the security at the door who don't read Lenni's tells the way I do.

Lenni barely crosses the threshold before Colby moves in, closing the gap. He wraps both arms around her waist, pulling her back against his chest as though he's been waiting for this all night.

My jaw clenches painfully. A hot rush floods my chest, like someone lit a match inside me.

Professional, I remind myself. Contractual. Observe. Don't react. But my hands curl into fists at my sides anyway.

Lenni returns a brief, light hug – camera-safe, headline-proof – then steps back on purpose.

Colby ignores the space, keeps one arm tight around her waist. I taste copper in my mouth.

"Missed you," he murmurs into her ear— loud enough to draw eyes, quiet enough to feel intimate. Loud enough for me to hear, which I'm sure isn't accidental.

She offers a measured smile and lets herself be steered toward the private bar.

Every step they take together feels like sandpaper against my skin.

That was the move that mattered—not the touch, not the hug, but the guiding.

Her body reacts predictably: a flicker of tension, shoulders stiffening, her smile tightening at the corners. She hates being led. I hate watching him lead her.

As they wait for her drink, Colby murmurs again—something about how stunning she looks, how she always steals the room. My fingers twitch with the urge to pull him away from her.

Lenni accepts her drink.

The glass sweats against her fingers. She watches the liquid for half a second longer than necessary —measuring, deciding. Not careless. Calculated.

She darts past him back to the U-shaped booth, sliding in at the end beside Sin—smart placement, an anchor at her shoulder. The relief I feel is embarrassing.

Kai takes the next seat, Ro and Blaize curved around opposite, as if the booth exists just for them. Colby settles at the far end, across from Lenni, like the table is his stage and she is his target.

I hang back—not close enough to catch every word, partly by choice, partly because I don't need to. I watch body language instead: Lenni's public smile, her eyes when she thinks no one noticed, her hands—still or fidgeting.

And Colby—always leaning, always pressing, playing protagonist even when he isn't the star. The night wore on in strobing flashes.

Ro laughs too hard at whatever Blaize says—either genuinely amused or turning her charm into a weapon.

Blaize leans in, eyes keen and curious, like Ro is a riddle he wants to crack with his teeth.

And Lenni…

Lenni drinks.

Not recklessly, not in a mess—just enough.

She slows between sips. Watches the room. Takes another anyway.

Enough for her edges to blur. Enough for her laugh to come easy when Colby leans in close. Enough for her cheeks to warm when his hand brushes hers. Enough that she drops her shoulders, armor slipping free for the wrong audience.

When I realize she's tipsy, something hot and ugly twists in my gut.

Without thinking I edge closer to the booth, clip my line of sight, sharpen my focus. My jaw aches from clenching.

Lenni glances my way, holds my gaze a beat too long –

Not asking. Not apologizing.

Just checking.

Like she wants to know if I'm still here.

– Then looks away like nothing's changed.

Like she doesn't see me burning alive in plain sight.

The DJ shifts into an easy beat and the girls get up to dance. Ro snags Kai's wrist; Sin trails behind, mock-annoyed.

Lenni hesitates. Colby does not. He's on his feet in an instant, hand out, full-on charm mode. "Come on, Len. Miami's not for sitting pretty."

Lenni rolls her eyes, but her mouth twitches. She rises, and my stomach drops as every head turns.

They move onto the small dance floor.

Ro owns it—hair flying, laughter bright. Kai lets herself enjoy the moment in silent rebellion. Sin dares the world to question her. Lenni sways too—measured, just enough to show she is part of it.

Then Colby slips in behind her, pressing close. His hands settle on her hips in the strobe lights.

Lenni doesn't push him off. She doesn't pull away either.

Not because she wants him. Not because she

doesn't.

Because she knows exactly what the room expects – and she gives it just enough.

She moves with him, expert performer, giving him what he wants.

Grinding, swaying, heat—a scene people would pay for.

Professional. Contract. It's for show.

And still, it feels like she knows exactly where I'm standing.

I stay rooted where I belong: watching, scanning for threats, telling myself that's all it is. But my eyes linger too long each time Colby leans close to her.

My throat tightens when she laughs at something he whispers—sharp and quick.

He beams like he's won something precious. Something that isn't his to win.

My hands curl into fists at my sides. I unclench them. Clench again. The contract in my head recites its cold terms: protect, don't possess. Professional boundaries.

I repeat them anyway, like saying it enough times might make it true.

Sin slides over to Lenni with a look that says she's done pretending. She leans into her and whispers something. Lenni's smile falters, then she nods. Relief floods through me like a drug.

Kai rejoins next, silent and vigilant.

Ro doesn't. She's pressed against Blaize, laughing low, making her choice. Lenni's brow lifts.

"Ro," she calls above the music.

Ro waves without looking. "Catching a ride with the Hollows!"

She doesn't call for me.

She just looks—once.

And my feet move like I've been trained by her silence.

"Okay," I say into my comms, steadying my voice. "We're moving."

Colby trails her back to the booth, his hand drifting to her waist. I imagine brushing it away. Instead, I watch her slide aside at the last second, Sin padding in beside her like a human shield. The satisfaction I feel when his arm drops empty is unprofessional. Dangerous.

"Leaving so soon?" he asks with a forced grin.

Lenni's polished smile returns. "Early morning."

"Miami doesn't do early," he shoots back.

She shrugs. "I do."

I step forward, placing myself between them without thinking. "Car's ready."

Her gaze warms just a fraction—maybe a trick of the lights, maybe the answer to every silent question I've been asking.

"Perfect."

Colby's grin tightens. "You always got him calling your shots?"

Her eyes go cool. "He calls exits. I call my life."

Colby laughs it off like a joke. It isn't.

The fierce pride that swells in my chest isn't in

my job description either.

The girls rattle on in the car just like always—defusing the night with sarcasm and gossip.

Sin gripes about the DJ. Kai gripes about the sloppy venue staff. They both poke fun at Ro, and Lenni snaps to her defense with that exasperated edge that portrays exactly how much she cares.

"She's fine," Lenni says, voice sharp.

"She's a menace," Sin shoots back.

Lenni's lips twitches. "That's why we keep her."

Kai glances at Lenni. "And what about you?"

"I'm fine," Lenni rolls her eyes.

Sin snorts. "Sure."

They move on to Colby—how he hovered over Lenni all night, how he was insufferable, how the tabloids will feast on this.

I stay silent, staring out the window as the city lights blur into streaks. My body feeling wrecked, my mind too loud, and all I want is a long shower, a soft bed, and a break from replaying the way Lenni had danced tonight—like she could ignite a room without ever getting burned.

I can still see Colby pressed against her back, his hands on her hips, her letting him look like she meant it.

But what matters most is the glance she shot me before we left the venue: not soft, not pleading—just there.

As if she needed to know I was steady. That I hadn't wavered.

We pull up to our building. I swing the door open. Lenni steps out, heels clicking, shoulders squared, chin held high—Lenni Vale, armor fully on. But as she heads for the lobby, her hand brushes my forearm for an instant—too fleeting to be accidental, and yet she doesn't look back.

I follow her inside, trailed by silent security and the distant hum of Miami. In that moment I realize I'm not just craving sleep. I'm bracing for the part of this job where pretending isn't protection anymore.

Colby is playing a dangerous game and Lenni is letting him.

Worse than the tabloids is knowing she started drinking just enough to blur her own rules. And worse than that is knowing I noticed.

Because noticing is a crack.

And cracks are how lines get crossed.

We reach her door. She fumbles once—just once—with the keycard before she catches herself and forces steady hands.

I shouldn't notice.

I do.

She gets the door open, then stops with her back to me, breath hitching like she's holding something down.

I wait for the usual: a joke, a barb, a dismissal.

Instead, she turns her head slightly—just enough for me to hear it.

"Don't let me make any more bad decisions tonight."

Then she disappears inside and the lock clicks.

And for the first time since I took this assignment, I can't tell if the threat is outside her door —

or already in the room with her.

CHAPTER 11

LENNON

Texas

Texas crashes over me like a hand pressing into the back of my neck.

The sky stretches too wide, the sun glares too bright, and our bus's AC fights a losing battle.

My skin can't decide whether it wants to sweat or combust.

Grits is sprawled in the aisle with his head on his paws, ears twitching every time the bus sighs or the driver taps the brakes.

And Hank—

Hank stands half a step away from my universe, like gravity took human form and opted for a plain tee.

No badge, no tactical gear, just those forearms, and that calm posture saying he could move in a heartbeat if he had to.

Approachable if you try. Dangerous if you don't.

The kind of stillness that makes everything else feel louder.

Which makes every instinct flare, even as my body stupidly relaxes in his orbit, craving the pocket of safety he creates without trying.

I hate myself for it.

My phone buzzes with an incoming FaceTime before I can spiral too hard.

MOM.

Hank's eyes flick to my phone. Not nosy—just aware. Like he files family calls in the same mental drawer as potential threats.

His attention shifts away immediately after, deliberate privacy, which somehow makes me more aware of him instead of less.

I accept the call before my mother starts texting in all caps.

Her face pops up, too close to the camera, glasses perched on her nose, hair half up.

"Lennon Marie," she says, in the tone she used when I was thirteen and she'd found a vape in my pocket. "Hi."

"Hi," I reply, instantly defensive. "Why FaceTime?"

"Because you missed my last three calls," she says, narrowing her eyes past the screen. "And because..." She tilts the phone, and I glimpse a tablet in her other hand.

Oh no.

"Mama"

She beams like nothing about my life scares her. "Who's this man I keep seeing you with?"

I freeze. "What man?"

She taps the tablet like it's affronted her. "The tall one. The one always hovering."

"He does not hover," I snap.

Across the aisle, Hank's mouth twitches.

My mom's eyes sharpen. "Ohhh. So you *do* know which one I'm talking about."

I inhale.

"Mom. He's security."

"Security?" she repeats. "Is that what we're calling him now?"

"Yes."

"Mm-hm." She leans in, voice dropping like she's about to share gossip with herself. "Because I saw that video. The one where that other boy, from Hollow Mesa, keeps getting in your space. And then your... security..." Her eyes flick upward, like she's mentally zooming in. "—steps in."

"He was doing his job."

She softens in that dangerous way.

"Baby, you sound steadier with him there. You look steadier."

The words land harder than they should. Like she's naming something I haven't decided exists.

Suddenly the bus feels silent.

Ro stops pretending not to listen. Kai's eyes open, just a slit. Sin's scrolling slows. Hank turns away, offering me privacy with his back.

I hate him for being considerate.

"I'm fine," I rush out. "It's literally his job."

Mom doesn't argue, just watches me like she reads beneath my makeup. "Is he nice?" she asks.

I laugh once, sharp. "Define nice."

She quirks an eyebrow. "Does he make you feel safe."

My pride rises like a shield.

My throat tightens. "He's doing a good *job*."

Her eyebrows shoot up. "That's new."

"Mom – "

"Lennon," she says softly, using my real name like a grounding wire. "I'm not prying. I just worry. I see those clips—strangers too close. I don't like that."

"I know," I mutter.

She sighs. "Are you getting any rest?"

"Sometimes."

She points at her tablet. "Are you dating that Mesa boy?"

My face contorts. "No. Apparently it's called '*Good Optics*'."

My mom's eyes widen. Then she smiles, slow and knowing. "Oh."

"Stop that."

"I didn't do anything," she says, innocent as a fox.

I drag a hand down my face. "Mom, please stop Googling me."

"I am not Googling you," she lies, immediately. "I am *researching.*"

Ro actually laughs out loud.

Mom glances sideways. "Who was that?"

"No one."

"Lennon," she warns.

I angle the camera to include Ro's grin.

"Hi, Mama."

Mom lights up. "Rowan! Tell my daughter to

stop being mysterious."

Ro's eyes sparkle. "She can't. It's a medical condition."

"Ro," I hiss.

Mom chuckles. "Okay. I'll let you go. But call me tonight. After rehearsal. And if that tall guy is around—"

"Mom."

"—tell him I said thank you."

I freeze. She softens. "Okay?"

I swallow. "Okay."

"Love you."

"Love you."

She ends the call before I can beg not to be alone with prying eyes. I stare at the black screen too long. Ro leans forward in a hush: "Your mom likes Hank."

"I'm going to push you into traffic," I whisper.

"Texas traffic's mean. It'd survive. You wouldn't."

Kai lets out an amused exhale. Sin shakes her head. I clamp my phone away. Hank finally looks my way—a quick glance, warm eyes asking, You okay?

I give him a jagged smile. "Don't."

He lifts one corner of his mouth. "Copy."

The word lands softer than I should.

Damn it, it helps.

Without thinking, I shift half a step closer—barely noticeable, just enough that his shoulder blocks the aisle behind me.

I don't register it until Grits lifts his head and settles again, like the world just corrected itself.

I don't move away.

Evie thinks this duet will set the tour on fire.

"Sex appeal moves tickets," she announces, fingers dancing across her phone screen like she's conjuring the heat wave. "The Lone Star State eats up romance."

Romance.

Like my actual life is just content waiting to be packaged, consumed, and discarded.

The moment our bus tires stop rolling, the vehicle transforms into a cramped studio.

Grits claims his spot in the corner, watchful as a chaperone. Ro stretches across the couch with her songbook, performing boredom while catching every word.

Kai and Sin stand against the wall, arms crossed, expressions unreadable.

Then Colby struts in, Stetson tilted just so, swagger turned on, that guitar case swinging from his hand.

"Vale," he says, voice dripping with familiarity.

I flash my stage smile. All teeth, no warmth. "Bridges."

His grin stretches wider. "Ready to break the internet again?"

"Ready to get through rehearsal," I counter, not giving an inch.

He edges closer—testing boundaries like always, measuring how much space he can steal before I make it awkward for everyone.

I feel Hank shift somewhere behind me – not stepping in, not retreating. Just there. A quiet line drawn without being announced.

His attention drifts past me.

That's when he spots Grits.

His expression sours. "Christ. Is that a rodent traveling with you?"

Ice slides down my vertebrae.

Grits' head pops up, ears alert – like he clocked a threat before I did.

Colby chuckles at his own joke.

"Thing looks like a meth-addicted chihuahua. Sure it won't take a chunk out of me?"

Around me, the temperature drops. Ro's gaze turns razor-sharp.

"We couldn't be so lucky." She seethes.

The smile stays on my face, but it changes – honey laced with arsenic.

"Colby," I drawl, voice smooth as Tennessee whiskey, "insult my dog again and we're going to have a serious problem."

His cocky grin slips a fraction. "Jus' playing around."

"I'm not." My tone remains melodic, pleasant

even.

The bus goes so quiet – silence that decides who holds power in a room.

Colby's throat bobs as he forces a chuckle.

"Shit. Message received." He raises his palms in surrender. "We good."

Hank remains motionless behind him, but his presence radiates—solid as a mountain at my back. He makes no move to intervene.

Doesn't need to.

He watches like he already knows how this ends – like he trusts me to hold the line.

He studies Colby with the calculating focus of a chess master memorizing his opponent's strategy.

Grits snorts once, dignity wounded, then rises and pads over to Hank, tail swinging in a hesitant pendulum.

Hank's fingers find the spot behind Grits' ears. Grits melts against him.

A perfect fit. As if Hank has always belonged here. As if this space has been his longer than I'm willing to admit.

I'm the first to break eye contact, annoyed at the relief flooding my chest.

"About that duet," Colby interrupts.

"Right," I nod. "The duet."

Colby keeps trying to make it flirty.

I keep making it performance.

Evie will call it chemistry.

The tabloids will call it romance.

Social media will call it something dumb and catchy. Whatever the internet thinks they deserve.

And I'll keep smiling until my cheeks ache and my consent gets blurry.

After rehearsal ends and the band scatters, I stumble upon Hank in the tour bus's excuse for a kitchen.

He's down on one knee with Grits' front paws claiming his thigh, my dog's stubborn body pressed against his chest like he's found his new favorite human. Grits' tail gives a single, decisive thump.

Something behind my ribs unravels before I can catch it.

I freeze in the doorway, watching them unnoticed.

Hank fills the space differently than anyone else—makes the already cramped bus feel steadier.

Like gravity settled instead of pressed.

His eyes lift and find mine.

No flinching. No covering. Just recognition like he knew I'd been standing here all along.

Heat crawls up my neck – caught in a softness I can't recognize.

I tilt my chin up, armor sliding back into place.

But Grits ruins it by climbing further into Hank's lap, shoving his head under that massive palm, demanding more attention.

Hank's smile breaks open—genuine and warm

and dangerously unguarded.

Without realizing it, I lean against the doorway instead of leaving. One breath. Two. Longer than I meant to stay.

My defenses crumble, my pulse steadies.

My skin remembers what trust feels like.

My body recognizes safety.

It's infuriating.

My pride demands I flee even as I breathe deeper than I have in months.

I turn and leave the room before I'm forced to acknowledge something dangerous:

That I've never felt as safe — not adored, not claimed — just… steady… as I do in the simple quiet of Hank Godfrey's company.

And that might mean nothing.

Which somehow makes it worse.

That realization? I can't afford.

Not now.

CHAPTER 12

HARLAN

Texas

Texas has bass in its bones.

These crowds make me nervous—they don't just show up, they swarm, hollering and sweating and ready to rush the stage if someone looks at Lenni wrong.

My hands haven't stopped checking my earpiece since we pulled up.

I'm doing my third perimeter sweep when I pass Lenni's dressing room.

Door's cracked. She's at the mirror—black eyeliner, that focused look she gets before shows. Armor on, piece by piece. Her shoulders square up when she catches my reflection.

She sees me watching. Doesn't say anything.

I don't either. Just give her a thumbs-up and a smile I hope looks confident.

We've gotten good at that.

That quiet check-in.

I should keep walking.

I don't.

Because somewhere along the way, I stopped checking on her just for the job – and started checking because she looks for me back.

Hollow Mesa exits in a thunder of applause as roadies swarm the stage—a choreographed frenzy of gear shifts and setup. Sweat slicks the floor. The air is thick with bodies and anticipation.

I position myself at my post—eyes tracking the crowd pit, monitoring both side passages, maintaining visual on the security line and all entrances.

Lenni steps out and the place detonates.

Every night, every town, it's identical—she appears and suddenly thousands believe salvation has taken physical form.

Tonight there's an edge to her. A precision.

Like she chose the burn instead of letting it choose her.

The perimeter holds. The crowd stays where it should. No wandering hands breach the boundaries.

Only sound. Only brilliance. Only warmth.

Only her.

I force myself to see her through a professional lens. Not as a woman, but as an assignment.

My pulse has other ideas.

"HOUSTON," Lenni drawls, stretching the word like she's dangling a dare.

The crowd answers with a roar, as if they've been starved for this moment. My pulse skips as I watch her eyes flick to the wings – then toward me.

Not asking for permission.

Just checking the line still exists.

Then she grins and says it.

"Y'all wanna make the internet mad tonight?"

Instant pandemonium. Phones shoot up. The pit surges. I clamp my shoulders down—not panic, just focus. Because I know exactly what's coming.

Lenni turns stage-right, crooks a finger like she's beckoning a storm.

"Get your ass out here, Colby."

The place goes feral.

Colby Bridges jogs out owning every inch of this chaos—hat pulled low, grinning, guitar already slung over his shoulder. He doesn't look at the band first. He looks at her.

My stomach twists – not panic.

Recognition.

He reaches Lenni, seizes her hand, lifts it as if they've won something together. My jaw clenches. I force myself to watch the crowd, the rails, the aisle—but my periphery never loses them.

Colby leans in, murmurs something in her ear. Lenni's smile holds; her posture stays loose. But her mouth tightens – just for a heartbeat.

The band hits their cue. The duet detonates,

and the crowd freaks out all over again.

It's PR gold—two stars, one stage, a "will they/won't they" tease that will make its way through every social feed.

Colby turns up the heat immediately. He closes the gap between them like it was choreographed—singing too close to her mic, tilting his body to corner her for the cameras, fingers grazing her hip in a spotlight-safe tease.

My heart snarls in my chest.

Lenni plays along. But just enough.

When he tries to pin her, she pivots into a spin—playful, untouchable—steps in one beat on the chorus because the crowd demands it, then slides out before it ever feels real. She holds herself an inch back from his lean; he presses to cross that line.

His verse drops low and intimate—eyes glued to her lips, like he's singing to her instead of with her. At the chorus, he leans in as if he'll brush her cheek with his voice.

My teeth grind. I don't flinch; I don't feed the fire. I just inch a half-step so I'm ready—in case the crowd lunges, or Lenni's smile cracks and she needs me.

Lenni lifts her chin, meets Colby head-on. Her voice stays steady, her smile sharp enough to cut glass. She serves the performance: heat, tension, the illusion of danger.

She never gives him her center. He keeps trying to take it.

But when her eyes flick to the wings—just for a split second—they find me.

And something inside me settles before I can stop it.

The duet crescendos on a perfect note.

Colby slings an arm around her shoulders like a victory lap. Lenni laughs it off, raises her hands, makes the moment look bigger than it is.

The crowd screams as if they've just seen the start of something real instead of a carefully scripted tease.

Colby drinks it in, bows, then leans in one more time—one more "accidental" brush, one more camera-friendly closeness.

Lenni steps back like water flowing around a rock. She points at him with the mic, cheeky and bright.

"Give it up for Colby Bridges, y'all!"

The audience erupts again. Colby winks at the front row then jogs offstage.

Lenni turns back to her band. The show doesn't miss a beat.

I exhale, tension melting into relief—and a warm pride I can't hide. She's mesmerizing. She's in control. And yeah, she might flirt with danger, but she always, always knows how to dance back to me.

Not to me.

Toward me.

She finishes the set like nothing happened.

Like her skin didn't crawl.

Like my molars didn't ache.

Houston gives them the clip they came for, and I give myself the only order that matters:

Stay professional. Stay sharp. Stay ready.

Because the danger isn't always in the crowd. Sometimes it's familiar hands and friendly smiles. Sometimes it's a man who thinks a woman's image is public property.

The penthouse suite is Houston glass and ego—floor-to-ceiling windows daring you to look away.

Marble so flawless a sneeze might crack it.

Texas is Hollow Mesa's turf: roadies hauling cables, crew in black T-shirts, and a clutch of "friends" who haven't lifted a mic but know where to find the good liquor.

Somebody's barefoot. Somebody's filming.

Then Lenni walks in with her band, and the room bends around her like gravity.

My pulse tightens. I press myself against the balcony's edge—two exits, a clear sightline, every muscle coiled. It's my job to watch her. It's also the only thing between me and wrecking the place.

Colby meets her at the threshold—of course he

does—with a smile.

He slides a hand around her waist, claiming her in front of witnesses.

My jaw clenches, but I stay.

Lenni shifts just enough to remind him she's not property. She's tired, the room is watching, Evie's voice echoing: Lean into it. Give them something.

He guides her toward the bar while I stay on the fringe, focus sharpening until it aches.

Lenni pours a light drink—more mixer than liquor—because control is her credo.

Colby watches, cataloguing every drop. He leans in.

"Hell of a show. You kicked ass. You and me up there? Solid gold."

She offers a polite smile. "It was a good moment."

He corrects her. "It was a great moment. We should really give 'em something to talk about."

Her gaze flicks to the phones, then to me.

Permission, or maybe apology—neither. Just checking the line still holds.

Colby laughs. "Your boy needs to relax."

My stance doesn't change, but every fiber of me tightens.

He lifts his glass. "Toast with me. To the duet."

Lenni hesitates half a heartbeat, clinks. "Cheers," she says, airy.

He gulps and leans lower. "I get it—your guard dog doesn't like me."

"Don't call him that," she snaps, and the word comes out sharp, roughened – edges dipped in Tennessee instead of polish. Her smile goes cold.

Colby smirks. "I'd be pissed off too if I had to sign a contract that kept my hands off you."

That's when my feet move. Not anger – recognition. I close the distance until I'm within arm's reach. Lenni's shoulders drop a fraction the second I'm there. Not weakness. Awareness. Her body acknowledging the line got tighter.

Colby sees me but keeps talking, drunk on his own boldness. He edges into her space, both hands on her waist.

Lenni goes still—not frozen or scared – controlled. Like a match goes quiet before it flares.

He laughs. "Come on, Lenn—"

"Colby," she says, low. "Back up."

He laughs. "It's just a kiss."

She says one word, cool and final: "No."

He leans closer. "C'mon. We've been coming on to each other for weeks."

Her eyes blaze. "I haven't been coming on to you."

He tries anyway.

She shoves him back.

The room fractures.

I grab his shirt – controlled, precise. No spectacle. Just stop.

"She said no."

"Chill, man."

"She's mine to protect," I say, clipped. "Even

from you."

Colby raises his hands, smirk faltering.

"Relax, man. She's yours to protect. Nothing else."

My grip tightens just enough. "Keep your fucking hands off of her."

He glances at the crowd, at the phones, at the angle shifting on him. "You're making this a thing—"

"I'm ending this thing." I step back two measured strides, repositioning him out of her space. Then I let go.

Lenni doesn't look back. She storms off—no stumble, no cry.

Just steel. I follow, giving her room but never more than an arm's length away.

In the hallway, the noise falls away. She breathes too fast; her fists are white at the knuckles. She waits until we're past the elevator, then turns.

"I knew this would happen."

I keep my voice soft. "I know."

She rubs her forehead. "Evie created this. I should've never let it go that far."

We walk to her room in silence. She doesn't speak again until the door clicks shut behind us.

I sweep fast—faster than usual, because my head is still full of Colby's hands on her waist.

When I finish, I turn.

Lenni stands in the entryway, shoulders squared like armor, but her eyes give her away

— too bright, too sharp, like she's holding herself together by will alone.

I step closer, careful.

"Are you okay?"

She lets out a sharp laugh that doesn't reach her eyes. "No."

A beat. Then softer, almost annoyed with herself, "I'm fine."

I don't argue.

Instead, I keep scanning the room, voice low.

"You don't need to shrink to make other people comfortable."

She goes still.

I continue, quieter:

"And you don't have to handle men like that alone while I'm standing here."

Her breath catches — subtle, but I feel it like a shift in gravity.

"This is my fault," she says finally, voice tight. "I agreed to the charade."

"No," I answer immediately. "He crossed a line."

She swallows hard, jaw flexing. "I shouldn't have let it get that close."

Then she looks at me — really looks — and something changes in the air between us.

Not softer.

Sharper.

More honest.

Her voice drops.

"We keep pretending this is just professional," she says slowly. "And it's starting to feel like a lie."

The words land between us like a match dropped in dry grass.

I swallow, caught off guard by how direct she is — by how badly I want to answer in a way that would ruin both of us.

Instead, I force my voice steady.

"Lenni…"

I don't finish the sentence.

Because finishing it would be crossing a line I'm not sure I could walk back from.

CHAPTER 13

LENNON

Texas

Texas heat is different.

Texas heat doesn't just sit on you—it *suffocates* you, and I'm already running on fumes.

Last night keeps looping in my head like a bad chorus I can't shake. Colby's hands and the way my skin went tight, instinct screaming before my brain caught up.

Then, Hank's voice, low and lethal, cutting through the noise when he told him to get his hands off me.

That isn't even the worst part.

It's the moment after, back in my room, when the truth fell out of my mouth like it was tired of being caged.

How can we keep pretending this isn't happening?

I hate that I said it.

I hate that it felt like relief.

I hate more that it was true.

My media obligation is at noon. I've slept four hours in two days and my emotions are doing donuts in the parking lot of my ribs.

Evie doesn't call. She never calls when she's angry.

She sends a voice memo.
I'm halfway through makeup when my phone buzzes.

Evie: *"Okay. Morning recap. Houston did numbers. The duet clip is outperforming projections—especially male 18–34. That's good."*

A pause. A smile I can hear.

"But last night got messy. We don't shove, we don't escalate, and we don't let security touch talent unless there's blood. We're pivoting to 'mutual energy, mutual respect.' I'll handle the messaging."

My jaw tightens.
She continues, tone still pleasant – still managerial, still polished:

"You did fine in the moment. Truly. But next time—let it breathe. Let me breathe. Texas likes heat, Lenni. Don't ice it out."

The memo ends with a soft chime.
No question. No check-in. Just correction disguised as praise.
That's when it clicks—Evie isn't mad Colby crossed a line. She's mad he crossed it where cameras could see it break.
Suddenly I understand something ugly:
They don't mind danger.
They just want it framed better.
I'm in denim shorts, a tank, boots—because everyone expects a version of me. Loud enough.

Sharp enough. A little dangerous.

Lately, I'm not sure which version feels more like a costume.

The real me never gets invited onstage.

The "Lenni Vale" they think they know.

My band is scattered around the green room like a pack of feral cats pretending they aren't protective—like they didn't wake me up last night after the Colby thing.

Hank had let them in, and Ro leaned into my doorway, voice too casual to be anything but serious. "You alive?" she said, eyes scanning me like she was checking for bruises, "or do we need to bury a man?"

Ro is stretched out on a couch with sunglasses on inside, acting like she doesn't regret her hangover. Kai perches on the armrest, doom-scrolling with her jaw clenched. Sin claims the corner like she's pissed off at the world.

And Hank—

He's in the hallway.

Not in the room. Not hovering. Just close enough that my body can feel where he is the way it can feel a storm coming – before the sky changes color.

That's the problem.

My body has started mapping him.

The podcast studio is cold in that manufactured way—air conditioning turned up like they want to keep everyone stiff and compliant. There's a tiny table, two microphones, a neon sign on the wall with a joke phrase that someone paid too much money for.

The host is shiny and charming.

We do the intro. The plugs. The "how's tour?" small talk.

I answer like I'm trained.

Because I am.

Then his grin shifts – there it is. The pivot. The bait hook sliding into the water.

"So," he says, leaning forward like we're sharing gossip over sweet tea. "We have to talk about what the internet is calling…"

He checks his phone, delighted.

"*Encore Entaglement.*"

My smile snaps into place so fast it could crack porcelain.

Somewhere behind the studio door, I feel Hank's presence go sharper—not moving closer, just.. more there.

I keep my voice light. Cute. The version of me people pay for.

"Please don't say that out loud again," I deadpan. "It sounds like a duvet brand."

He laughs too hard. "Okay, okay—but—He lifts a finger like he's being polite. Like he's not about to jab straight into a bruise. "Are you dating Colby Bridges?"

The bait question they've been dying to clip into a fifteen-second loop with captions and drama music.

My pulse doesn't show on my face.

It does under my skin.

I tilt my head like I'm thinking. Like this is cute.

"Colby and I are on the same tour," I say. "Does that count as dating now? Because if so, I'm also dating my drummer, two stage managers, and at least one venue security guy who keeps yelling at people for climbing railings."

The host laughs again, pleased like he got something.

"But the videos—" he presses. "The chemistry. The duet. The way you two—"

"The way we *performed*," I correct smoothly, still smiling. "You know. That thing musicians do. On a stage. With a crowd. And cameras."

He raises his hands like he's innocent. "I'm just asking what everyone's asking. Is this a tour romance?"

Tour romance. Like it's a trope. Like it's not my actual life. My stomach is tight. Because last night wasn't a "moment." It was a man with liquor on his breath trying to take something I didn't offer. It was Hank's voice going cold and final.

My smile stays. My stomach turns.

"If I ever have something to share," I say brightly, "I promise I'll do it in a way that makes the internet lose its mind properly."

He cackles. "So that's a no comment."

"That's a 'my work is my work,'" I say, voice sweet as poison. "And my personal life is…

mine."

For the first time, the words don't feel like a defense.

They feel like a boundary.

He tries one more time, because they always do.

"Okay, but—your bodyguard. People are obsessed with him. Is he jealous? Protective? Is he —"

I don't even blink.

"Is he doing his job?" I offer. "Yes."

The host laughs and pivots, because he can tell I'm not giving him blood and he's got other questions on his little list.

He tosses out something about tour rituals, my favorite fan sign, "craziest DM you've ever gotten." He tries to steer back toward romance twice, but I keep slipping the leash. I give him jokes. I give him charm. I give him the polished version of me that knows how to survive a room without letting anyone touch the soft parts.

Inside, something is boiling so hot it could burn through bone. It's not just the podcast. It's everything.

The label that wants heat. The PR team that wants a story. The tabloids that want a romance. The fans that want a fantasy. Colby acting like he's entitled to a starring role in my narrative.

I'm in the middle, smiling through it because every time I don't, it becomes a headline. It becomes a fight. It becomes a punishment.

When they finally cut, the host shakes my hand like we're buddies and tells me I handled it "like a pro." I smile like that doesn't make me want to bite him.

"Awesome," I say. "Can't wait to never do this again."

He laughs, thinking I'm kidding.

I'm not.

I stand, thank the producer, wave at the intern who looks like she wants to be me and doesn't understand the cost yet, and then I walk out before my composure loosens enough to be a problem.

And there he is.

Hank in the hallway like gravity.

Not rushing. Not dramatic.

Just steady. Quiet. Creating a pocket of space where I can breathe without the world trying to climb inside my mouth.

My throat tightens at the relief of it.

I hate relief. Relief makes you soft. Relief makes you need.

But this isn't need the way Evie means it.

This isn't dependency.

This is my body recognizing the difference between being watched and being guarded.

"You good?" he asks.

He doesn't step closer.

Doesn't reach for me.

Just angles his body slightly so no one walks between us.

Like he already knows what I need without making it a conversation.

"I didn't set anything on fire," I say.

His mouth twitches. "Proud of you."

Something in my chest unlocks – not because it's approval.

It's recognition.

"I'm a model citizen."

"Debatable," he murmurs, and there's something in his tone—warm, familiar—that makes my shoulders loosen like it recognizes home before my pride can veto it.

Ro comes out behind me, snapping her sunglasses down. "If he says 'Duet Entanglement' one more time, I'm suing the internet."

Kai follows, expression tight. Sin last—quiet, eyes scanning, still carrying that post-Colby edge like she hasn't set it down since last night.

Hank shifts immediately—subtle, automatic—placing himself so the hallway stays clear, so we aren't boxed in. Like he's moving furniture in a room only he can see.

We head toward the exit as a unit—me in the middle, the band flanking, Hank and the rest of security creating a moving perimeter that makes strangers unconsciously step back.

Even in the afternoon, the heat is thick. It sticks to skin. It makes you feel like you're breathing through fabric.

We're halfway to the car when my phone buzzes again.

Evie: *Good job deflecting. Clips are clean. We'll reframe the narrative around "artistic chemistry" and "strong boundaries." Austin will be smoother.*

Strong boundaries.

I almost laugh.

Because boundaries don't mean much when someone else decides where they are.

Hank opens the door for us and we slide in.

As we pull away, Ro launches into a dramatic recap. Kai groans. "They're already cutting clips."

Sin stares out the window. "We need to stop feeding it."

Ro turns to me. "You did good though. You didn't give him anything."

"Because if I give them anything," I say, voice too calm, "they take everything."

The car goes quieter at that.

Even Ro's mouth shuts for a second, which is basically a miracle.

Hank rides in the front seat with the driver, not part of the conversation but still in it—the way he always is.

Like he's listening without listening. Like he's there without taking.

We get back to the hotel, and the lobby is all marble and chilled air and people pretending they don't recognize me while absolutely recognizing me.

Hank and security walk us inside looking casual to anyone who doesn't know what to look for.

I know what to look for now.

I know the way Hank shifts when someone gets too close. The way his gaze flicks to exits. The way his shoulders square without him thinking about it.

I used to track every exit myself — doorways, corners, reflections in glass — counting escape routes like breathing. Tonight I don't realize I've stopped until we're already halfway across the lobby.

My posture loosens before I catch it, shoulders dropping, guard slipping without permission — like my body forgot it's supposed to stay ready when he's doing it for me.

And I hate that my body relaxes when he does it.

Because I'm not choosing to trust him anymore.

It's just happening.

We make it to the elevators, and I can already taste sleep. I can already picture my bed. My room. The dark. Silence. The kind of quiet that doesn't ask anything of me.

"One more night," Kai says, half to herself. "Then Austin."

Sin exhales. "Festival weekend."

Ro rolls her shoulders like she's gearing up for war. "Two days of sweaty strangers trying to touch our girl."

I make a face. "Love that for us."

The elevator dings. We step out onto our floor.

The hallway is quiet, carpet swallowing footsteps. My door waits at the end like sanctuary.

Hank pauses at my door.

"Tomorrow," he says, voice low. "We'll adjust the plan for Austin. More bodies. Tighter lanes. You'll have an out at all times."

My chest aches with the urge to say something stupidly honest.

Thank you. Don't leave. I hate that I need you.

Instead, I lift my chin. "I'm going to sleep for every minute I'm allowed."

A smile tugs at his mouth. "Good."

They peel off toward their rooms. Hank hangs back a beat longer, eyes on me like he's checking the edges of my mask.

"You want me close tonight?" he asks.

It's simple. Professional.

But there's a softness under it now. A recognition. Like he knows what the world did to me today, and he's offering a buffer without making me ask for it.

So I do the thing I never do. I tell the truth in a way that won't kill me.

"I need air," I say.

His eyes warm. "Okay."

And before my pride can snatch it back, I add— quiet, fierce, like I'm daring myself –

"I need you."

The words land between us like a live wire. Hank doesn't step closer. Doesn't take advantage. Doesn't turn it into something I'll regret.

He just shifts his weight — grounding himself instead of moving toward me.

Matching my space instead of closing it.

"Copy that," he says softly.

And I hate myself for how my body calms at the sound—like my nervous system just got permission to stand down.

Because I'm not angry about rumors.

I'm angry that everyone keeps mistaking my silence for permission.

Standing here in this hallway, in Texas, with Hank holding the line without ever crossing it — I understand something I've been circling for years:

I don't want the noise to stop.

I want to decide what it means.

And for the first time in a long time,
I'm not pretending I don't know the difference.

CHAPTER 14

HARLAN

Texas

Everyone's quieter than they were two days ago.

Partly because Texas heat drains you and partly because the last time Lenni said *I need you,* she acted like she was furious at herself for meaning it.

I'm not supposed to carry that sentence with me. I don't know where to put it, so I keep it anyway.

I can't convince myself it doesn't mean something – so I carry it anyway.

Austin isn't a venue. It's an entire ecosystem.

A festival is a crowd with teeth—too many entry points, too many wristbands that look real, too many people who think access is a right because they paid for it.

The air is hot and sweet with sunscreen and fried food, but underneath it hums with something I don't trust.

We roll in and it's immediate chaos.

Golf carts weaving, crews hauling cases, stage managers barking into headsets. Press is already filming like the show started hours ago. Fans are stacked along fencing, eyes bright, waiting for the chance to breathe the same air as her.

Lenni moves through it like she was made for the noise.

That's what kills me.

She's five-foot-two and built like a blade—compact muscle, stubborn heartbeat, eyes that dare the world to touch her. But crowds don't care about size. They only care that she's *Lenni Vale*.

I'm stressed before we even hit the backstage corridor.

Mila's voice crackles through comms.

"We're running tight. Keep her route clean."

"Ten four," I say, and keep my posture relaxed while my brain builds maps in real time.

Kai, Sin, and Ro stay close, the band moving in a practiced cluster. Security fans out behind them. I keep myself where I can see the angles and still keep Lenni in my peripheral.

Peripheral isn't enough anymore, but it has to be.

She's in festival gear—denim, boots, the kind of top that looks effortless and definitely wasn't. Sunglasses shoved into her hair. That *don't try me* face already loaded.

She catches me watching her once.

Her mouth tilts like she's satisfied with it.

Then she just says, "This is going to be disgusting, isn't it?"

"Probably," I answer. "Try not to lick anything."

She snorts, and the sound is small—real—like it slips out before she can stop it.

The sound hits somewhere low in my chest before I shut it down.

We make it to the side-stage holding area. The first act is finishing. The crowd is surging toward the barricade.

A staff member approaches too fast.

I step once—just once—and they stop short like they ran into an invisible wall.

My hand lifts slightly behind Lenni without touching her, instinct already preparing to redirect if needed.

I don't raise my voice. I don't need to.

"Credentials," I say calmly.

They fumble for their lanyard, cheeks flushing. It's legit. I let them pass with a nod.

Lenni's gaze flicks to mine, and for a second I can tell she's irritated… and relieved.

She hates that she's relieved.

I love that she doesn't have to say it.

As we shift forward, my fingertips brush lightly at the small of her back — not guiding, just confirming she's still exactly where I expect her to be.

That's the thing about a pro: even when the world is chaos, she finds the pocket and owns it. She steps into the lights and the crowd becomes hers. She talks to them like she's known them forever. She bites. She grins. She gives them the version of Lenni Vale they came for.

I step closer than necessary as the noise spikes, positioning myself just off her shoulder without thinking — correcting it a second later like the instinct slipped too far.

The band is tight. The set lands hard.

I don't relax. I don't get to.

After the set, the route back to the trailers should be controlled. It isn't.

Festivals create bottlenecks, staff shifts, gates opening and closing. The crowd gets impatient and starts pushing like entitlement is a force of nature.

We hit the narrowest corridor—a temporary fencing lane that runs between the stage and the vendor row. It's the only direct path back without doubling our time, and right now it's packed with people who shouldn't be there.

I see it before we're in it.

Hands already reaching through the fence.

Phones out. Faces bright with hunger.

Someone shouts her name and the sound triggers the rest of them.

"LENNI!"

Lenni's shoulders tense.

Something tight pulls in my chest with it — fast, instinctive, too personal for protocol.

Her band tightens around her, instinctive. Ro is already scanning for the fastest way to create a diversion. Kai's jaw clamps. Sin's eyes go flat in that way that says she'll bite someone's fingers off if they reach too far.

Mila's voice in my ear: "Harlan, reroute if you can."

I look at the corridor, look at the crowd, look at the fencing that's meant to be a barrier and is currently just… a suggestion.

No time for a reroute.

Crowd control's gone to hell.

I make the call in a half-second.

"Clear space," I snap, sharper than usual — the command landing like a dropped blade.

I whip around to Lenni, hands already reaching for her.

"Up," I say — low, final, leaving no room for argument.

Her eyes widen. " Excuse me?"

"Lenni," I bark, voice steady but urgent – the tone that says danger without saying danger. "Up. Now."

Her eyes flash, lightning-fast, but there's no hesitation – just blind trust.

She moves without question, and that trust hits harder than the crowd ever could.

She steps in close. My hands seize her hips. I hoist her skyward like she's made of air, muscles burning with the surge of adrenaline as I lock her onto my shoulder with precision.

The gasp that tears from her throat hits my ear.

Her fingers dig into my shoulder, nails biting through fabric as she hisses, "Drop me and I'll haunt you until your grandchildren feel it."

"Not happening," I growl.

Failure isn't an option when she's in my hands.

We cut through the chaos – a bullet through flesh.

The crowd erupts.

They lunge forward, a writhing mass of desperate hands clawing higher, fingers stretching for any piece of her they can claim.

I twist my body violently, creating a human fortress between her and the fence line.

Instinct overrides training — not possession, just protection.

Security swarms us, but all I feel is her heartbeat hammering against me and the singular mission pounding through my veins: protect her at all costs.

Then we move – fast and controlled, a straight line through the gauntlet.

"Hands to yourselves!" Ro snaps. "She doesn't know where you've been!"

Someone laughs. Someone keeps reaching.

Lenni stays still above me, compact and rigid. She's trying not to make it worse, trying not to feed the frenzy. But her hand is gripping my shoulder hard enough I'll have bruises.

I don't think about how her leg fits my grip.

I think about getting her out.

We clear the corridor in under thirty seconds, but it feels like a minute underwater.

The moment we hit a controlled zone, I lower her carefully. Her boots touch ground, as she steadies herself.

She doesn't move right away.

The noise of the crowd fades behind us, but the adrenaline doesn't. It sits heavy in the air between us, sharp and electric.

Her weight leaves my arms and my body notices immediately.

My jaw is clenched.

She's closer than she should be. Close enough that I can see the pulse in her throat, fast and wild.

Lenni looks up at me — eyes bright, not frightened exactly, just... aware.

For a second, neither of us speaks. The world narrows to breath and space and the absence of chaos.

Her hand is still on my shoulder.

She realizes it at the same moment I do.

Her fingers loosen slowly — not rushed, not embarrassed — just deliberate.

"You always do that?" she asks quietly, voice rough from adrenaline.

I blink. "Do what?"

Her mouth twitches like she's trying not to smile.

"Turn into a human battering ram."

A breath leaves me that almost sounds like a laugh. "Only when necessary."

She studies me like she's recalibrating something she thought she understood.

Around us, the band moves, security talks,

radios crackle — but for a moment it feels distant.

She exhales slowly.

"Thanks," she says, quieter now. Real.

I nod once, because anything more would feel like stepping somewhere neither of us is ready to go.

She steps back first.

The air shifts with it.

Night One ends with her safe, but I'm wired and on edge. Adrenaline that won't fade.

Back at the trailer lane, the band is buzzing. Lenni's laugh is quiet—real—like she forgot the internet existed for a second.

I watch it like it's something precious. Like it's something someone might try to steal.

My phone vibrates.

A runner approaches at the same time—young guy in a delivery polo, carrying a tall white box.

Flowers.

My body goes cold so fast it's almost calm. The runner smiles, breathless.

"Delivery for Lennon Vale?"

I step into his path before he can take another step.

"Who's it from?" I ask.

He glances down at his clipboard. "Uh… it just says 'anonymous.' But it's paid for."

"Company?" I ask.

He points to the logo on his shirt. It's a local service—legit enough on the surface.

His hands shift on the box – tight grip, then loosened. Nerves. Or guilt. I catalog both.

My eyes go to the box, then to his hands.

Then to Lenni—laughing with her band five yards away, unaware.

I keep my voice level. "Set it down. Step back."

The runner hesitates. I don't change my tone. I don't raise my voice. I just let the air in my posture tell him I'm not negotiating.

He sets the box down slowly. I move it away from the group—two steps, three—creating distance.

"Thank you," I say. "You're done."

He swallows and nods and backs away like he finally realized whose world he wandered into.

I watch him go longer than necessary, committing his walk, his shoulders, his face to memory.

I kneel beside the box. I don't open it right away. I check the seams. The weight. The tape. The smell—chemicals, fuel, anything that doesn't belong.

Then I find the envelope taped to the side. Simple cream paper. Neat handwriting.

The tape is fresh. The edges clean. Not shipped days ago. Delivered recently. Recently enough that whoever sent it knew she'd be here tonight.

My stomach tightens. I slide a finger under the flap and open it carefully.

The card inside is plain.

The message isn't.

**YOU LOOK PRETTY WHEN YOU THINK YOU'RE SAFE.
I LIKE THE SONGS ABOUT COMING HOME.
DON'T FORGET WHO YOU ARE WITHOUT THE LIGHTS.
—I'M STILL HERE.**

The noise dulls and the world narrows.

This isn't about access anymore.

This is about her.

Every exit re-maps itself in my head. Every risk recalculated.

They didn't just learn the tour schedule. They watched her – watched for the moment she relaxed.

I close the card and stand. My face stays neutral. My pulse doesn't.

I don't bring it to Lenni. Not yet.

Not in front of her band. Not in front of the crew. Not in front of anyone who will panic and make her panic.

I turn and find Mila. She's at the edge of the group, already watching me like she felt the shift. I hold the card low at my side and walk to her. When I'm close enough, I keep my voice quiet.

"Mila," I say.

Her eyes flick to my hand. "What is it?"

"Threat," I answer. "Direct."

Her expression doesn't crack. "Show me."

I hand her the card, she reads it once, then again, slower.

When she looks up, her eyes are steel. "Night Two?" she asks.

I don't hesitate. "Cancel," I say.

Mila nods once, decision made. "I'll handle the messaging. Keep her calm."

"Always."

She tucks the card away and then she turns back toward the group, already wearing the face she uses when she needs to make a crisis look like a scheduling change.

I watch Lenni across the space.

She's laughing at something Ro says, head tipped back, shoulders loose, eyes bright.

For a second, she looks like she's just a woman with her people.

Not a headline. Not a target.

Not a story everyone wants to own.

My chest tightens.

Because someone is trying to ruin this.

And they're not aiming for the stage anymore. They're aiming for her.

And if they think they're going to reach her—
If they think they're going to touch her—

I feel something cold settle behind my ribs.

The contract is ink.

But this?

This is the part of me that doesn't wash off.

I keep my face calm and my posture loose as I walk back toward her. Steady and warm on the outside.

But inside—

I'm all teeth.

CHAPTER 15

LENNON

California

My second night of the festival gets canceled without drama.

Mila calls it *logistics*. Evie calls it *a strategic pivot*. The statement online makes it sound like the universe politely rearranged itself for everyone's comfort.

I know better.

This is someone putting a hand between me and the edge before I even realize how close I was.

We load up like nothing happened.

Texas falls away behind us in shimmering heat. The highway turns into scrubland and open sky, landscape that makes you feel small.

Inside the bus, everyone's quiet in that post-adrenaline way.

Ro is sprawled sideways on the couch, sunglasses pushed into her hair. Kai rides the line between checked out and hyper-aware, one earbud in, one out. Sin scrolls with that unnerving calm she gets when she's clocking threats instead of posts.

Hank stands half a step outside my orbit.

No tactical vest. No badge. Just a plain tee, those forearms and that posture that says *I could move if I needed to – but I won't unless you make me.*

My body hates how safe that feels.

Hates it because it remember safety too easily.

Grits is stretched in the aisle like he pays rent.

Then he crawls forward and wedges himself against Hank's boot like it's instinct instead of betrayal.

Hank glances down, scratches behind Grits's ear without thinking, and my stomach does something embarrassing and uninvited.

Like my nervous system just picked a side without asking me.

Kai's phone buzzes. She reads whatever's on the screen and her jaw tightens. "There's another tabloid push."

Sin doesn't look up. "Of course there is."

I don't know what it says.

I already know the shape of it – me flattened into something clickable.

My phone vibrates.

Evie. Another voice memo.

I don't play it out loud. I don't need to. I already know it'll say *don't panic*, *let it breathe*, *let them talk*. Like silence is the same thing as control.

Ro exhales sharply. "He's not backing off. He's just… switched tactics."

Sin's thumb stills. "Predators adapt."

Kai looks at me. "You okay?"

I smile. It's the public one—sharp, polished, dangerous.

"I'm fantastic," I say.

Kai winces.

I lean back and add, casual as a threat, "If they want a villain arc, I can deliver."

Silence settles—not concern, not pity. Respect.

The desert miles stack up.

Sun bleaches everything. Gas stations blur past like placeholders. The bus turns into its own small universe—tight, humming, unavoidable.

And inside it, my awareness of Hank sharpens instead of fading.

Not big things.

Small ones.

A brush of his fingers when we both reach for the same bottle of water – neither of us pulling away immediately, the contact lasting just long enough to feel intentional before we both remember ourselves.

A glance held too long after Ro says something feral and I laugh before I can stop myself.

His gaze drops briefly to my mouth before lifting back to my eyes, like he caught himself mid-thought.

A quiet joke meant only for me.

He doesn't look at anyone else when he says it.

When the bus shifts over a rough patch of road, his hand lifts automatically, hovering near my elbow like he's ready to steady me — even though I don't actually need it. He lowers it a second later, like he realized.

It's the first time in a long time my chest remembers how to unclench without bracing for impact.

By the time we cross into California Evie is already texting about Malibu like it's a gift. An extra day, soft light, the ocean. *Reset.*

Reset—like I'm a device you power down when the system overheats.

The Malibu house is glass, soft linens and expensive quiet. Salt air drifts through the open doors, but even here, I can feel the internet waiting.

I step onto the balcony anyway. I need air that belongs only to my lungs.

The ocean stretches wide, sky bruising pink at the edges. For one honest second, I pretend I'm just a girl standing in the wind.

And then my body calls bullshit.

Footsteps behind me—not loud, or rushed – measured. A heavy rhythm my nerves recognize before my brain catches up.

I know it's him before I know why I know.

Leather and salt and something clean—cedar soap, sun-warmed skin, the faintest trace of gun oil he never seems to carry on his hands but always has somewhere in his world.

Hank.

I don't have to look. My senses clock him the way they would clock danger.

The soft scuff of his boot, and the pause he always takes at a threshold. The subtle pressure shift when his size enters the space behind me.

He stops at a respectful distance—close enough to be real, far enough not to trap me.

The wind shifts and his shoulder brushes mine lightly before he steps half an inch back — like the contact surprised him too.

"Perimeter's locked," he says softly. "You're clear."

I nod, staring out at the water like it's the only thing that can keep me steady. Then, without turning, I say, "The girls want to do a beach fire tonight."

He doesn't hesitate. "Not a good idea."

Not control, just factual.

I smile to myself—sharp, satisfied. There it is. The cage.

I turn, heat flashing under my ribs. "I don't want to be managed tonight."

His jaw tightens—but his voice stays even. "It's not secure."

I turn, heat flashing under my ribs. "You know what else isn't secure?"

He stays still. Let's me have space. Let's me have my moment.

"My life," I snap. "My privacy. My body. My name."

I lift my chin, eyes bright with something mean. "So if I want one hour where the only headline is *Lenni Vale eats a burnt marshmallow and tells the world to kiss her ass*, I'm taking it."

Silence stretches—tense, charged. Hank exhales slow, controlled. Not a sigh. Not a correction. A recalculation.

"Okay," he says. "Then I'll make it safer."

The fight drains out of me so fast it almost feels like vertigo.

I blink. "You'll... what?"

"I'll adjust. I'll coordinate security," he continues calmly. "Wide coverage. You get your fire. You get your night."

I don't say it often. He doesn't make it heavy.

The fight in my chest stutters – confused by being heard instead of handled.

"Thank you," I say, quieter.

He nods once, like it's just another part of the job. Like my freedom matters as much as my safety.

Grits trots onto the balcony and immediately presses against Hank's leg like the verdict's already in.

I shake my head. "Unbelievable."

Hank's mouth quirks. "Truth teller."

"Clearly questionable taste," I mutter, but my smile sticks.

I step closer to the railing without thinking — and realize a second later I've stepped closer to him too. Close enough that our shoulders nearly touch when the wind shifts.

I look back out at the ocean, heart pounding with something reckless and bright.

My hand rests on the railing — and his moves there a moment later, fingers brushing lightly against mine before either of us reacts.

Neither of us pulls away immediately.

The contact is brief, accidental... and somehow louder than anything we've said tonight.

He shifts first, subtle enough it could mean nothing.

I pretend it did.

He didn't try to win. That might be the most dangerous part.

Downstairs, the house is all white counters and ocean-view calm, until the girls turn it into a war room in under a minute.

Ro barrels into the kitchen first. "I'm declaring this a spiritual necessity."

Kai opens the fridge. "We have—" she pauses, unimpressed, "—a suspicious amount of kale."

Sin appears behind her, already holding a bottle of sparkling water. "Who bought kale?"

Harper pops up from her laptop, phone in hand. "The rental comes stocked. They think we're going to juice cleanse."

Ro makes a gagging sound. "Over my dead body."

I lean on the counter, watching them scatter. Hank's still nearby – I can feel him the way you feel heat from a stove you're pretending not to touch.

Ro starts pulling items from the cabinets.

"Okay, we need: chips, something sweet, something salty, something that says we're adults even though we are not."

Kai finds a pantry shelf. "Crackers."

"Boring," Ro declares.

Kai holds up a box. "Artisan crackers."

Ro squints. "Fine. Bougie boring."

Harper holds up a bag of marshmallows like she hit the jackpot. "These came with the place."

Ro gasps dramatically. "The universe does loves us."

I reach for the marshmallows before Ro can hog them. "We need chocolate and graham crackers."

Kai slides open a drawer. "Found them."

Ro points at her like she's proud. "See? Tactical. This is why you're my favorite."

"I am not your favorite," Kai says flatly.

Ro grins. "That's exactly what my favorite would say."

Sin finds a cooler in the closet and drags it out—then starts tossing drinks into it. Waters and sodas. Then she raids the mini bar.

Ro spots them. "Are we drinking?"

Sin's gaze is dead calm. "We're decompressing."

Harper lifts her phone. "I'll bring the speaker."

My chest loosens another notch. This – this is what life is supposed to feel like. Not cameras. Not headlines. Not men with entitled hands. Just… snacks and friends and the ocean.

Hank appears in the doorway like he was summoned by my exhale.

He's dressed casual to try not to capture attention – plain tee, worn shorts, nothing that announces authority.

That steady, measured stance still gives him away.

He scans the room once — quick, quiet, efficient — then his eyes land on the cooler.

His eyes flick to me first. Always me first. Then everything else.

He steps aside and speaks into his comms, voice low. "Two teams. Wide perimeter. Blend. No cluster."

Ro leans toward me, whispering loudly, "Blend," like she's tasting the word. "He's so hot when he's bossy."

"Ro," I warn.

She lifts her hands. "I'm shutting up. I'm shutting up."

No one believes her.

Least of all me.

A few minutes later, we're moving out like a group of criminals trying to look casual.

Hoodies, hats, and sunglasses. "Undercover" that fools no one, but it makes us feel better.

Security trails at a distance—spread out, not clumped. Hank walks slightly behind me, giving me space.

Close enough that I can feel him without seeing him. Far enough that no one could call it possession.

We reach the sand from our beach access house, and the world opens up—wide, darkening ocean, a smear of sunset clinging to the horizon, the sound of waves like a slow exhale.

My shoulders drop before I realize they've been tight all day.

Ro drops the blanket, then Kai starts arranging snacks. Sin sets the cooler down and scans the beach.

Harper cues up the speaker, volume low—Ella Langley singing *"Please Excuse The Mess"*, softly, not drawing attention.

I kick off my shoes and let the sand swallow my toes.

Behind me, Hank shifts position again – not stepping closer, just… aligning himself with the edge of the world.

The shift is small, almost invisible, but it places him between me and everything behind us without ever crowding my space.

I look at him over my shoulder. He's wearing less than I've ever seen him wear – no armor, no utility, just muscle and calm.

The thought of seeing him naked hits me uninvited.

He meets my gaze like he's answering the question I didn't ask.

I'm here. You're safe.

My throat tightens.

His eyes flick briefly to my mouth before returning to mine — controlled, deliberate, like he's correcting himself.

I turn back to the ocean before anyone can see it on my face.

Ro recruits one of our security details to start the fire, and the first flare of warmth punches through the dusk.

For the first time in days, I let myself sit in it. Let myself breathe. Let myself exist.

And somewhere behind me, in the rhythm of waves and low music and crackling fire, Hank holds the line—quiet and steady—like he always does.

Even when I don't ask, he reads the shape of my fear and builds himself around it.

He never reaches for me—and somehow, that's what makes it dangerous.

The fire pops. Laughter drifts. The ocean keeps its endless secrets.

I realize the truth with a clarity that steals my breath: If this goes any further, it won't be a scandal that ruins me.

It won't be the tabloids or Evie and Colby or the internet sharpening its knives.

It will be the way my body already knows where Hank is—the way my heart keeps choosing him long before my mouth ever would.

I am standing on the edge of something irreversible, and for the first time in my life—I don't step back.

CHAPTER 16

Harlan

California

Lenni Vale is standing on a beach in Malibu, in a bikini top and cutoff shorts like she owns the night.

Like the ocean rose just to watch her breathe.

She tilts her head at me with that look—half challenge, half please—the kind that makes a man forget where his boundaries live.

Firelight kisses her skin, throwing gold across her collarbones. The denim rides low on her hips, frayed threads brushing bare thigh. She's barefoot, red cup dangling loose from two fingers, hair up in a messy knot that won't stay contained.

Every instinct I have clocks it as a bad idea.
Every instinct I have refuses to look away.

"C'mon, Hank," she says, lips tipped into a grin that could talk a man into sins he'd never confess. "It's just a bonfire. Everybody's here."

Everybody being Ro, Kai, Sin, Harper, and a handful of crew, and locals I've already cataloged twice.

Three exits. Two blind spots. One drunk guy pretending he's not watching her. Another pretending he doesn't recognize her.

I log all of it without moving my face.

"Crowds, alcohol, fire," I say flatly. "That's three strikes."

She steps closer, heat and smoke and Lenni wrapped into one dangerous package.

Close enough that the warmth from her skin cuts through the ocean air, close enough that I have to consciously keep my hands at my sides instead of reaching.

My pulse spikes like my body thinks this is a threat.

It isn't.

That's the problem.

"You don't have to be on all the time," she says softly. "You're allowed to have fun."

That's the lie.

Because even when I try—even when I force my shoulders to loosen and my hands to unclench—I never stop watching her.

Never stop tracking the space between her and everyone else.

She drinks more than she should.

Not sloppy or reckless. Just enough to soften the edges she normally keeps sharpened like weapons.

She laughs louder than usual, leans into Kai's side, then Sin's.

She sits cross-legged on a log, head tipped back, throat bare in a way that makes my stomach twist with both desire and dread.

My brain notes vulnerability. My body notes

something else entirely.

I hate both.

And I let it go longer than I should. I shouldn't. But I do.

Because she looks… free. And who am I to take that from her?

Until she doesn't.

It happens quietly. No stumble. No scene. Just Lenni going slack mid-laugh, head tipping back, eyes glassy when she looks up at me.

My job and my heart pulling me in opposite directions.

"Okay," I murmur, already moving, hating myself for it. "That's enough."

She squints at me like I've offended her personally. "You're bossy."

"You're drunk."

She considers that, then shrugs. "Fair."

When I lift her, she doesn't protest. Just loops an arm around my neck and sighs like she's been waiting for permission to stop holding herself together.

Her fingers slide briefly along the back of my neck as she adjusts, the touch absent-minded — and my grip tightens a fraction before I catch myself.

She's lighter than she should be. Warm. Soft in a way she never lets herself be when she's sober.

I shouldn't notice these things.

I notice everything.

Her cheek presses into my chest as I carry her

bridal-style back toward the house, firelight fading behind us.

Her breath slows against me, syncing without effort, and for one dangerous second I let myself feel how easily she fits here before I shut that thought down.

My heartbeat quickens traitorously.

"I knew you'd take care of me," she mumble. "Always knew."

My jaw tightens.

"That's my job," I say.

The words sound like a lie I've told too many times.

She hums, unconvinced. "No. You choose it."

That lands deeper than anything she could have said sober.

Inside the house, everything is quiet and dim. I navigate by memory, muscle, and instinct.

When I set her on the edge of the bed, she looks up at me, eyes soft, unfocused.

I should look away.

I don't.

A loose strand of hair falls across her face. My hand lifts automatically — then stops midair, curling back into a fist before it reaches her.

The motion is so instinctive I barely recognize it until I'm already pulling back, like my body moved before my brain remembered the rules.

"Do you have anyone back home?" she asks suddenly.

The question lands heavier than it should. I

could lie. Should lie.

"No," I answer.

She nods like she's filing that away.

"Figures." A pause. Then, teasing and tender all at once, "You're making me soft, Hank."

She reaches up before I can stop her – before I can even decide if I want to stop her – and presses a slow, careless kiss to my cheek. Not sexual. Not innocent either. Just… intimate.

Her fingers linger against my jaw a second longer than necessary before falling away, like she forgot to let go.

My brain goes white.

Every instinct screams: don't move.

Every other instinct screams: take her mouth.

I want to turn my face.

I don't.

Because she's drunk. Because she trusts me. Because if I break that trust, I lose something I can't get back.

My chest tightens, breath going shallow. Every instinct I own pulls in opposite directions—toward her, away from her—until I feel split clean down the middle.

My hand lifts again without permission, hovering near her shoulder like I'm about to steady her — or hold her — before I force it back to my side.

Instead:

"Maybe I'm just softening the parts that've been too hard for too long."

Her eyes flicker.

Then footsteps.

Relief and disappointment hit me at the same time.

Kai appears in the doorway with Sin right behind her, both of them taking in the scene in one glance.

Their eyes flick from Lenni to me to the space between us — assessing, measuring, understanding more than I want them to.

"Get some sleep," I say quietly, stepping back before I forget who I am. Before I become who I want to be.

She smiles, already drifting. "Night."

"We've got her," Kai says gently.

I nod once and leave without looking back.

Because if I look again, I know I'll stay — and staying feels like crossing a line I won't be able to uncross.

Because leaving feels like ripping something out of my chest.

Because if I stay, I might stop pretending this is just a job.

And staying would ruin everything.

Or save me.

The house is dim, bonfire glow leaking through the windows in soft orange bands. Somebody left a lamp on in the living room.

I clear the first corner and see Blaize, leaning against the kitchen island like he belongs there, shoulders loose but eyes too keyed toward the hallway. He's trying to look casual but failing. The tension in his stance gives him away.

Ro. Of course.

I stop where he can see me without letting him close the distance.

My body squares without conscious thought — widening my stance just enough to own the space between him and the hall.

The same instinct that positioned me between Lenni and danger now locks into place here without hesitation.

My training runs ahead of emotion. Emotion runs right behind it.

My body does what it's trained to do—reads his hands, his weight distribution, his breathing. No weapon visible. No agitation. Just… anticipation.

"Didn't know we had visitors," I say.

Blaize's gaze snaps to mine. Quick assessment. Then a half-smirk like he's heard enough about me to feel brave.

"Relax, man. I'm not here for trouble."

"That's not how it works," I answer, voice level. "You don't get to decide whether you're trouble."

Silence stretches a second longer than comfortable. He feels it.

He gives a short breath that might be a laugh. "I've never given you any trouble."

His eyes flick—again—toward the hallway. It's an instinct he doesn't even try to hide.

"You waiting on Ro?" I ask.

His jaw flexes once. "Yeah."

After all this time. I've seen the way Ro looks at him when she thinks nobody's watching—like she's furious she cares. Like he's a bruise she keeps pressing to see if it still hurts.

I nod once, then move on.

Because I can't afford to linger in anyone else's romance when mine is currently a moral landmine.

Because watching someone else choose their risk feels too close to watching myself lose control.

I do what I always do when my head is too full: I work.

Perimeter first, then doors and windows.

I step outside long enough to scan the yard and tree line. Quiet. Distant laughter from people still lingering near the heat in the fire pit.

I check the empty rooms and flex space. Behind doors, under cushions, inside closets—because if Colby decided he wanted to be a problem, he wouldn't kick the front door in.

He'd smile. He'd joke. He'd act entitled to space that isn't his.

And entitlement doesn't take "no" well.

I check every extra room twice.

Then a third time without admitting to myself why.

No Colby. No stray crew. No drunk idiot sleeping it off in the wrong place.

Only quiet. The low creak of the house settling. And my pulse refusing to.

I stop outside Lenni's door.

On the other side, I hear voices—low, steady, female. Kai and Sin. They're in there with her. They stay a long time.

Long enough for the guilt to tighten around my ribs. Because I can't pretend I'm only rattled by the alcohol.

I'm rattled by the kiss. By the way she'd leaned into me like it was instinct. By how my body responded before my brain could slam the door.

By how her fingers felt against my skin long after she pulled away.

She was drunk.

That fact keeps flashing like a warning light behind my eyes.

Drunk means vulnerable. Drunk means uninhibited. Drunk means she doesn't get to consent to anything the way she would sober.

And I will die before I become another man who mistakes vulnerability for invitation.

I sit on the couch in the flex space outside her room. Close enough to hear her door. Close enough to move fast if anything goes wrong. Far enough to give her privacy.

The door finally opens as Kai steps out first. Sin follows, hair falling loose, posture relaxed like she's leaving a battle she won. They both spot me immediately.

Kai's mouth tilts. "Well. Look at that."

Sin folds her arms, eyes bright with amusement. "He's posted up."

I keep my voice steady. "She okay?"

Kai's expression softens a fraction.

"Yeah. She's gonna sleep."

Sin's gaze sweeps over me—slow and sharp—like she's reading the shape of the night on my face. Then she smirks.

"We talked about you," she says, like she's tossing a match onto gasoline.

My jaw tightens. "Did you."

Kai leans against the wall, voice light.

"Mm-hmm. Like… an embarrassing amount."

Sin adds, sweet as a hornet, "Lenni says you're —what was it—" she squints like she's searching her memory on purpose, "—'annoyingly steady.'"

Kai nods solemnly. "Her exact words."

Sin's grin widens. "And then she said you smell good."

My breath catches before I can stop it. Heat crawls up the back of my neck like betrayal.

My body betrays me—just a fraction. A shift. A tightening in my shoulders.

They both catch it.

Kai's eyes sparkle. "Oh."

Sin points at me like she just won something. "There it is."

I force my face into neutral. "She's drunk."

Kai's smile gentles. "We know." Then she pushes off the wall and starts down the hall. "Get some sleep, Hank."

Sin follows, then pauses and looks back over

her shoulder.

"For the record," she says, "if you break her, Ro will bury you."

I don't blink. "Noted."

Sin's mouth quirks. "Goodnight, golden boy." Then they disappear into the dark.

The hall goes quiet again.

And I'm left on this couch with my own thoughts—my own rules—my own stupid, inconvenient feelings.

I stare at Lenni's door. At the small strip of light under it.

I close my eyes for a second, just long enough to let the conflict bite down.

Wanting her.

Respecting her.

Protecting her.

Not confusing those things—because confusing them would ruin us both.

My hand presses briefly to the spot on my cheek where she kissed me before I drop it like the contact burned.

I open my eyes again and keep watch on the door.

Like a guard.

Like a penance.

Like a man who just realized the most dangerous thing on this tour isn't the crowd—

It's the way I'm starting to care.

And the worst part?

I don't want to stop.

CHAPTER 17

Lennon

California

I wake to the sound of movement. For a second, my body tenses. I don't remember agreeing to company. I don't remember –

Then the night drifts in, slow and fragmented – firelight snapping in the dark, someone laughing, my own voice too lose, too honest. Hank's arms under my knees. His chest solid against my cheek.

And then – my mouth near his skin. The press of my lips to his cheek.

My stomach flips.

Not regret. Not exactly. Just the sharp awareness that I crossed a line I don't usually let myself even look at.

I sit up, sheets tangled around my legs, and my head clearer than it should be.

I try to chase the memory past the kiss – try to remember what he said after. Something steady and gentle.

A sentence I can't fully catch, like it's floating just out of reach. But the feeling of it stays.

Like safety. Like permission. Like something dangerous I almost let myself believe.

I drag on an oversized T-shirt and pad down

the stairs, following the smell like it's a lifeline.

There's a man in the kitchen I don't recognize. Late forties, maybe. He has an apron on and groceries spread across the counter. He's chopping vegetables with practiced ease, moving like somebody who's done this a thousand times.

I stop short. "Uh – "

Hank looks up instantly from the table.

And my nervous system settles before my brain catches up.

He's already dressed. Boots on and coffee in hand. His posture relaxed but alert in a way that makes me unclench without asking permission.

When his eyes find mine, something my chest steadies.

He stands, unhurried, like he's careful not to startle me—even though I'm not a deer. Even though I've never been the type to spook.

"Morning," he says, voice low.

His eyes flick briefly to my face — searching, measuring — like he's checking for regret before letting himself relax.

I glance back at the man. "Who is that?"

Hank stands, unhurried, like he's careful not to startle me—even though I'm not a deer. Even though I've never been the type to spook.

"Chef Morales," he says. "He's here to prep meals for the week. He'll be gone in about thirty minutes."

I blink. "We... have a chef?"

"You do," he answers. "Temporary. Groceries

and prep only."

"I didn't know about this."

"I know," he says simply. "Mila arranged it this morning."

Of course she did.

My mouth goes tight, half irritation, half resignation. "Okay. Just—surprised."

Hank nods like that's fair. No judgment. No lecture. Just... acceptance.

He moves to the counter and pours coffee into a mug the way I like it—cream first, no sugar—and slides it toward me.

No asking. No fuss.

Just knowing.

His fingers brush mine as I take it — brief, accidental — but neither of us pulls away immediately.

"Thanks," I murmur, wrapping both hands around it.

The chef keeps working, respectful and quiet. Hank sits back down across from me like he's trying to make himself smaller than he is.

We eat eggs and toast off real plates.

The silence isn't awkward. It's just... full.

Full of everything I almost said last night. Full of the way Hank looked at me when I couldn't stand straight. Full of his hands steadying me like I was precious and not a problem.

I keep catching myself staring at his cheek.

At the place my mouth touched.

Wondering if he felt it.

Wondering if he's pretending it didn't happen.

His expression stays neutral, but his jaw is tight in that way that tells me he's thinking too hard. Or holding something back. Or both.

Footsteps thump down the stairs.

Ro appears first, hair a wreck, and eyeliner smudged. Blaize is right behind her, shirt wrinkled, a little too close, like the space between them got erased sometime last night.

I grin before I can stop myself. "Ooooh."

Ro flips me off without heat. "Shut up."

Blaize ducks his head, smiling like he doesn't regret a damn thing.

Hank doesn't react. Doesn't comment. Just sips his coffee, solid and quiet—like he's the kind of man who can witness chaos and not become part of it.

Like he's the kind of man who could hold a drunk girl in his arms and not take what she didn't mean to offer.

That thought hits sharp and warm all at once.

And maybe more dangerous than desire is trust.

When breakfast ends, the chef packs up containers, labels everything neatly, and slips out with a polite nod. The house exhales with him.

The door clicks shut.

And suddenly it's just us again.

I stare into my mug, then look up at Hank. "Can you take me to the beach today?"

The words come out softer than I intend. Not

weak—just honest.

"I need sunshine," I add. "Salt. Quiet."

I need space where I don't have to perform.

Hank studies me for a beat, eyes steady.

Then he nods once. "Yeah. We can do that."

Relief hits me so hard it makes my throat sting.

Upstairs, I change into a simple bikini – nothing fancy – black top and bottoms with cutoff shorts.

But I catch myself in the mirror and think of last night—think of Hank's voice, low and careful, saying something about softening what's been too hard.

I don't remember the exact words.

I remember the way they landed.

Like he saw the parts of me I usually hide behind stage lights and sarcasm.

I pack a cooler with sandwiches, fruit, waters. Throw in sunscreen. Ice. Napkins. The basics.

I'm halfway through zipping it when the memory of my own voice flashes—too loose, too sincere.

Do you have anyone back home?

Heat crawls up my neck.

I should be embarrassed. I should regret it.

I don't.

If anything, the only thing that makes my chest tighten is the idea that he might've heard it as a problem instead of a truth I didn't mean to hand anyone.

When I come back downstairs, Hank's changed too.

Swim trunks and a fitted black tee. A tactical backpack slung over one shoulder.

He looks… unfair.

Not in a pretty-boy way. In a steady, competent, dangerous-if-he-has-to-be way.

I pause on the last step. "You're really doing this."

He lifts a brow. "Doing what?"

"Letting today feel normal."

His mouth twitches. "I said we could go to the beach. I didn't say I'd stop paying attention."

I roll my eyes, but it doesn't have bite. "Maybe you'll let loose a little."

He opens the door for me, sunlight spilling in bright and unapologetic. "We'll see."

The house sits right on the water.

Not perched above it or hidden behind dunes —*on* it. The beach stretches out wide and pale, the ocean rolling in lazy, glassy waves.

We don't stay close.

I grab the bag and he grabs the umbrella and the cooler. We walk barefoot, sinking into cool sand, wind tugging at my hair, Hank matching my pace without crowding me.

Always there. Never pressing.

Every time I slow, he adjusts without thinking — our shoulders nearly brushing more than once before we both subtly shift away.

The farther we push across the sand, the more

the world falls silent – until all that's left is the roar of the surf and a pair of gulls squabbling overhead.

No footprints. No voices. Just us, swallowed by the beach.

I drop our towels first, stakes hammered into the soft dune, then fumble with the umbrella's ribs. Hank sets his pack down, eyes sweeping the horizon out of muscle memory before he eases onto the sand beside me. The sunshine glints off the waves, but my pulse refuses to calm.

Last night I gave him a tenderness I don't spare for anyone else. He didn't waste it – he held it like something precious. And now my mind spins: what if I need more? What if I'm asking too much of him?

On a reckless impulse, I scoop a handful of damp sand and hurl it at his shin. Grainy and cold against his skin—petty, desperate, perfect. He winces, blurting, "Really?" I flash him a wicked grin and bolt.

Adrenaline crashes through my veins, setting every nerve alight. Hank's on me in two strides—light, relentless. The salt-heavy air scorches my lungs as I veer toward the dunes, but he corners me, and I fling myself onto his back, clinging like a lifeline.

He gasps, then laughter tumbles out of him as he stumbles under my weight.

His hands settle on my thighs automatically — steadying, protective — and for a second neither of us moves, both aware of the contact before pretending we're not.

My heart hammers so hard I'm sure he can feel it against his back. I press closer, cheek against the heat of his skin, hair whipping into my eyes. Fear and exhilaration coil together in my belly, raw and electric.

We crash onto the warm sand, a tangle of limbs. He looms over me, arms braced either side of my head. The world narrows to the taut line of his jaw, the flicker of something burning in his eyes.

Between us, the air crackles. I don't think. My instincts take over: I tilt my face upward and brush a single, searing kiss across his lips. His breath catches in his throat; for one suspended heartbeat, the world goes still.

He pulls back, voice rough with control. "I don't want you making mistakes," he murmurs.

My chest tightens so fiercely I can't tear my gaze from his. "You're not a mistake," I whisper.

The words hang between us heavier now — not drunken impulse, not confusion — something chosen.

Hank freezes, as if I've shifted the entire axis of his world. He exhales, eyes searching mine for proof. "If anyone saw this," he growls low and half-amused, "I'd burn Malibu to the ground."

I laugh—thrilled and trembling all at once. "Dramatic."

"Accurate."

He slides off me, leaving a patch of cooling sand where his warmth bloomed. I sit up, dusting grit from my legs with shaky fingers, heart still drumming its wild refrain. When he shifts, I notice the unmistakable taut line straining against the navy fabric of his swim trunks – his careful distance betrayed by his body's honest response.

We lie back down on our towels, side by side, staring out at the endless blue. Silence stretches between us, charged and fragile. Something's changed—something electric pulses beneath the surface, daring us to acknowledge it.

I close my eyes, the sun scorching my face, but inside my chest a storm rages. Fear and longing twist together like a rope I can't untangle.

It's different now—not awkward or tense, just... honest. The wind tugs at my hair, the sun warms my skin. I squeeze sunscreen into my palm and slowly smooth it over my arms and shoulders, grounding myself in every deliberate stroke.

Hank keeps his eyes on the horizon until I glance up and catch him shrugging off his shirt in one seamless motion. His muscles gleam in the light, a sharp V leading down into the waistband of his trunks. My throat goes dry; I wrench my gaze away—probably too late.

He grabs the sunscreen and applies it with that same efficient grace he brings to everything. His skin catches the salt air as my pulse trips over itself.

I clear my throat. "Want some help with your back?"

He hesitates for a heartbeat, then nods. "Yeah."

He turns, offering his shoulders without a second thought. My hand hovers, then presses against warm, solid skin.

His breathing shifts slightly under my touch — deeper, controlled — like he's bracing without pulling away.

I spread lotion across him—each sweep careful, each movement heavy with meaning.

My thumb pauses briefly at the base of his neck before I force myself to keep moving.

His muscles shift under my touch—neither pulling away nor leaning in, just... existing. His back maps years of holding steady when everything else threatened to collapse.

I'm cautious, not lingering where my fingers could betray me, not rushing out of fear. Still, the air feels charged.

The ocean murmurs behind us, and a gust of wind lifts my hair against his shoulder. My forehead almost brushes his back and I freeze, aware of how easily this could tip into something irreversible. I finish and step back, rubbing excess lotion into my palms.

"All set."

"Thanks," he says softly.

He turns away, and I'm grateful for the space—while hating that I need it.

The salt-tinged air feels raw, like every defense I carry has been peeled back one layer too far.

After a moment, Hank breaks the silence. "Where'd you grow up?"

I blink at him. A normal question. "A small town in Virginia." I shrug ike it doesn't matter. "You?"

"Virginia, too," he answers. His mouth tips like he almost smiles – like the coincidence feels bigger than he's letting on. "You miss it?"

The question lands sharper than expected. I stare out at the water. "Sometimes I miss who I was before I knew better." I pause. "But I don't miss feeling trapped."

Hank nods like he understands that in his bones.

He nods slowly. Not polite agreement — recognition. Like something in my answer fits into a place inside him that's already shaped for it.

Another quiet stretch settles between us.

"My sister would've lost her mind if she knew I came down here with you today." He says suddenly.

"Your sister?" I turn toward him, surprised by the shift.

He chuckles, almost embarrassed. "Yeah. She's a huge fan."

Warmth blooms low in my chest before I can stop it.

"Casual fan or 'tattooed lyrics on her arm' fan?" I tease.

He smiles — really smiles this time, softer around the edges.

"Casual. Mostly."

"Mostly?" I press.

He looks out at the sea, voice softening.

"She introduced me to your music. Said you make people feel seen." A beat. "She wasn't wrong."

The air shifts – heavier, quieter.

I swallow.

"What's her name?"

"Emerson. Emmy." His jaw softens when he says it. "She'd kill me for giving her full credit."

"Emmy," I repeat. "How old is she?"

"Twenty-three. Too smart. Too stubborn. Thinks she can change the world if she argues hard enough."

I laugh. "Sounds familiar."

He tilts his head, eyes warm. "Yeah. It does."

I lie back under the umbrella, staring up at the sky.

"My mom would probably cry if she saw me doing this."

His brow lifts. "Doing what?"

"Relaxing," I admit. "Letting someone else handle things."

He doesn't interrupt. He doesn't reassure. He just stays – and somehow that makes it easier to keep talking.

"My dad left when I was little."

His jaw tightens.

"My mom stayed," I continue softly. "She's gentle in a hard world. Loves too much, forgives too fast. She really tried."

He listens without pity—and somehow that feels more intimate than comfort ever could.

I stare at my sandy hands and the words slip out before I can stop them. "What about your dad?"

He stills.

The wind keeps moving, waves breaking steady and endless, but beside me he goes completely quiet.

Then he exhales.

"He died young." He says finally. "Heart—fast, no warning."

My chest tightens.

"I'm sorry."

He nods once, gaze fixed on the horizon.

"One minute he was here," he adds quietly. "Next there was just the space he left behind."

I feel that emptiness in my own ribs. His gaze drops to my mouth for a flicker — then pulls away like it burned him.

I shift so our shoulders brush—accidental enough to deny, deliberate enough to matter. He doesn't move.

We sit like that, the ocean stretching in front of us, stories resting between us like fragile offerings neither of us knows how to hold.

After a while, he reaches into the cooler and hands me a bottle of water.

Such a small thing.

But it feels like care.

And for the first time in a long time, I let myself believe this:

maybe being safe doesn't mean surrender.

Maybe it can feel like salt air and sunlight.

Someone steady beside you — not holding you still, just holding the line so nothing else crosses it.

And maybe what scares me most isn't losing control.

Maybe it's wanting to stay.

CHAPTER 18

Harlan

California

I should feel relieved.

Lenni got her beach day without anything going wrong. No crowds or strangers pressing too close. No strangers testing boundaries. No hands reaching where they shouldn't.

Just sun, salt, and quiet.

Just her laughing – really laughing – a sound that breaks loose without warning and makes everyone around her forget to breathe for a second.

And that's the problem.

Because the moment she offered to sunscreen my back, something shifted.

Not outward. I didn't lean into it. Didn't touch her wrong. Didn't blur the line.

But inside?

Inside, something moved I can't file under protocol.

A line crossed without footsteps.

I keep replaying it as we walk up from the beach—her hand on my bicep, steady and warm, fingers grounding without asking permission. Her breath close enough to feel without trying. The way my muscles tightened under her touch like my body had its own opinion about what I deserve.

She's the one moving toward me now.

Not the other way around.

And somehow that makes the guilt worse.

Because if she's choosing it – if she's stepping closer willingly – then the only thing standing between us is me.

And I'm not sure I want to be the barrier anymore.

We crest the dune and the house comes into view, bright and loud and completely at odds with the quiet we just left behind.

Music thumps from somewhere near the patio. Laughter carries over the wind. A splash, then a shout.

People.

Too many people.

Lenni slows beside me, gaze sweeping the yard like she's taking inventory. Her mouth tightens.

"Tell me you didn't invite half the tour over," she murmurs.

"I didn't invite anyone," I say, but my eyes are already moving—counting bodies, tracking movement, clocking exits.

"Mm-hmm," she says, dry. "Still not thrilled."

I don't answer the feeling part of that. I answer the security part.

"Stay where I can see you."

She scoffs like she hates the words, but she doesn't argue.

That's the thing about her—she pushes, complains, tests the edges.. and then trusts me anyway.

We step fully onto the property and the scene hits me like a live feed.

Ro and Blaize are in the pool together, laughter sharp and easy, their bodies angled toward each other like they forgot the rest of the world exists.

All My Ex's Live in Texas by George Strait is blaring on a Bluetooth speaker. Sin and Kai stretch across loungers, sunglasses on, calm and watchful – predators resting, not relaxing.

Harper sits in the shade with her laptop open, one hand typing, the other wrapped around a drink, foot bouncing like she's pretending she's off duty.

And scattered across the yard—Hollow Mesa's guys, a couple crew members, and at least one unfamiliar face I flag immediately. Cornhole boards set near the side fence. Beer cans sweating in the heat.

My brain goes clinical.

I hate it.

Lenni's hand brushes mine as she moves ahead – barely there, almost accidental – then disappears like she caught herself crossing a line she doesn't want named.

My fingers curl reflexively after hers leave, like my body expected her to stay.

She glances back once.

Do your thing.

So I do.

I peel off toward the perimeter without making it obvious, checking gates, fence latches, the side yard, the blind corners where someone could hide and wait.

Nothing disturbed.

Still doesn't mean safe.

I swing back toward the patio and catch the second layer — two additional security guys posted near the side entrance, radios clipped, eyes moving.

They clock me and nod.

"Any issues?" I ask quietly.

"Quiet so far. Mila said it was cleared."

"Cleared doesn't mean clean," I answer automatically.

He smirks like he's heard that before. "Copy."

We sync comms. Confirm exists. Vehicles and coverage.

Routine.

Control.

The only thing keeping my head from drifting back to the way her fingers felt against my skin.

When I turn toward the yard again, Lenni is stepping down the patio stairs.

Right toward Colby.

He's leaning near the cornhole boards, beer in hand, posture loose like he owns the air around him. Not as pushy as before – but testing.

Always testing.

He spots her and his whole face lights up.

"Vale," he calls. "There you are. We thought you bailed on the fun."

Lenni's smile switches on—precise, controlled, polite enough to pass scrutiny.

It never reaches her eyes.

"I was at the beach," she says simply.

Colby chuckles, stepping closer by a foot.

"With *him?*" His gaze flicks toward me – quick, assessing.

My shoulders stay loose. My stance stays open. I don't escalate.

But I shift half a step closer without realizing it – subtle enough to read as positioning, not possession.

Lenni doesn't shift toward him.

Doesn't give ground.

Doesn't look at me either – like she refuses to let this become a triangle.

"He's my security, Bridges."

The words land flat and final.

The title hits harder than it should.

Somehow it feels like distance.

Colby's grin tightens before he smooths it out.

"Right," he says lightly, like he's unbothered.

He lifts his beer. "We're doing a little tournament. Cornhole. Winner gets—"

"No," Lenni says calmly.

Colby's grin falters, then recalibrates.

"C'mon, don't be like that."

"I don't play."

"Just one game. For me."

The phrase hits wrong.

For me.

Like her boundaries are negotiable currency.

Lenni's eyes narrow, patience gone.

She doesn't retreat. Doesn't flare.

She just turns away – clean and decisive – straight inside the house.

No apology. No explanation.

Colby watches her go, jaw flexing once, then glances toward me like he wants a reaction.

I give him none.

Just a steady look that says: *I see everything.*

His smile fades a fraction before he turns back to the cornhole game like he's not bothered.

But he is.

I track him until he's reabsorbed into the group, then shift my attention back to the door Lenni disappeared through.

Because the truth is, I'm not worried about Colby's ego.

I'm worried about mine.

About the way my body reacted when she touched me.

About the way the beach made me forget — just for a second — that I'm supposed to be a wall.

Not a man.

And I'm worried most of all because she's the one stepping closer now.

Because she's finally crossing toward me.

And if I'm not careful…

I won't step back.

I'll meet her there.

The flex space hits me first—and I stop short.

My things are gone.

Backpack. Boots. Shirt I'd tossed over the arm of the couch. All of it.

My pulse ticks up automatically, scanning for threat before thought catches up. Nothing overturned. Nothing disturbed. No signs of intrusion.

Just absence.

Then I hear it.

The shower.

Water running steady from Lenni's room.

I move carefully through the space, checking doors as I go, habit stronger than curiosity, until I reach the bedroom that was assigned to me when we arrived.

My things are neatly placed there.

Backpack against the wall. Boots by the dresser. Shirt folded over the chair like someone wanted it out of the way—not discarded, not careless.

Moved.

Deliberately.

I stand there longer than necessary, trying to

figure out who would do that—and why.

There's only one person who would do this.

And only one reason.

She didn't want my presence visible here.

Not hiding me. Protecting me.

I exhale slowly and return to the flex space, lowering onto the couch.

I wait.

Because rushing toward whatever she's setting up feels like losing control.

The shower cuts off and silence settles. I count without meaning to.

Thirty. Sixty. Ninety.

Then, I stand and knock once.

The door opens.

Lenni stands there in short, soft pajama shorts and a thin cami— damp skin glowing from the shower, cheeks flushed from sun and heat. Her hair hangs loose, dripping, curling at the ends.

She looks softer than I've ever seen her.

More real.

I clear my throat, forcing my eyes back to her face. "Did you move my things?"

"I did," she says easily.

No apology.

No hesitation.

Then she reaches forward and takes my hand.

Just like that.

Warm fingers wrapping around mine before my brain can decide whether to pull away – as she tugs me gently inside, shutting the door behind us with a quiet click.

Her thumb presses lightly against the inside of my wrist – grounding, deliberate – like she's checking if I'm really here.

"Why, Lenni?" I ask quietly, keeping my voice stead., "What are you up to?"

She steps closer, close enough that I feel warmth before touch. Soap. Salt. Something uniquely hers.

"If your things are in the room you're assigned to," she says, voice calm and deliberate, "then everyone will believe that's where you are too."

My jaw tightens.

"Yes," I say, low. "Because that's where I should be."

Her gaze lifts slowly to mine – not challenging, not teasing.

Certain.

"I think you and I both know," she says softly, "that's not where you want to be."

The air tightens between us.

Electric. Fragile.

My hand tightens around hers before I realize I'm doing it — not pulling her closer, not stopping her — just holding.

She steps back just enough to breathe, creating space instead of trapping me.

An exit. Always an exit.

That's what undoes me – not the invitation, but the freedom to refuse it.

She gestures toward the bathroom.

"Bring what you need. Shower here."

I don't move.

She watches me, not pushing, not persuading — just waiting.

"I'm going to read while you decide," she adds, already turning toward the bed like she hasn't just dismantled every boundary I've built.

No pressure or seduction, just an invitation.

And that's what breaks me.

Because she didn't corner me.

She trusted me to choose.

I stand there, heart hammering, mind racing.

I can still say no, walk out. I can reset the line.

But the truth settles slowly into my bones:

I don't want distance.

I don't want to pretend I don't feel the way she steps closer every time she's scared or tired or just… honest.

And for the first time since I took this job, I let myself imagine what happens if I stop pretending this is only professional.

I exhale.

And step inside.

I don't step in because she asked.

I step in because she didn't — because she trusted me to choose her anyway.

CHAPTER 19

Lennon

California

I tell myself I'm calm.

I'm stretched out on the bed with my book open, sunlight bleeding through the curtains, the quiet hum of the house wrapping around me like this is any other evening. Like my heart isn't beating just a little too fast. Like I'm not listening—really listening—to every sound behind the bathroom door.

The shower runs steady.

I read the same paragraph three times and don't absorb a word of it.

This could work, I think.

That's the dangerous thought.

That we could have this—quiet, contained, ours—and keep the rest of the world out. That it could exist without breaking anything.

Because it's only fair, isn't it?

I've spent my whole life holding myself up alone. Carrying. Protecting. Being the one who never leans.

If I want this—*him*—why shouldn't I take it?

The water shuts off and my pulse jumps.

I keep reading. Or pretending to.

The door opens and Hank steps out, towel low

on his hips, damp skin catching the fading light before he disappears briefly into the other room.

When he returns, he's wearing nothing but basketball shorts, bare feet silent against the floor.

He looks… stripped down in a way that has nothing to do with clothes.

He doesn't look at me right away.

He sits on the edge of the bed, forearms braced on his thighs like he's grounding himself against something heavier than gravity.

Suddenly I see it clearly – the hesitation, the restraint.

The way he's holding the line even when it hurts him to stand there.

Not afraid of me, afraid of what this means.

I know then that if I don't move, he won't. He'll sit there all night, choosing discipline over desire until it cuts him open from the inside.

So I close my book, and set it gently on the nightstand.

I rise onto my knees.

The mattress shifts as I crawl toward him, slow and deliberate – giving him every chance to stop me.

He doesn't move.

When I reach him, I wrap my arms around his middle from behind, pressing my body to his back.

Warm. Solid. Steady.

He inhales sharply, like he wasn't prepared for

how much that would undo him.

My cheek rests between his shoulder blades. My fingers curl lightly against his stomach.

Not demanding, just there.

"Lenni," he murmurs—my name low, careful, more warning to himself than me.

I tighten my hold instead.

My body fits against his back like it's always known where to go. Heat. Muscle. The solid reassurance of him holding still because he's choosing not to move—not because he doesn't want to.

"I know," I whisper. "I know you're trying to be good."

His hands flex against his thighs.

"I don't want to hurt you," he says quietly.

"You won't," I answer. "But if you keep pretending you don't want this.. you're hurting both of us."

Silence stretches.

He turns slowly, carefully, like sudden movement might shatter us.

His hands hover at my waist. Not claiming, asking.

I nod, and that's all it takes.

He leans in mouth finds mine with a smoldering insistence—not rough, no rushed – just a searing, full-bodied claim he's been starving to make. I gasp into the kiss, nails digging into his shoulders as the lines of his muscles melt beneath my touch.

We kiss like we've been aching for this forever.

Like this was inevitable.

He drags me closer, one hand pressed flat against the small of my back, the other curling around my jaw to hold my face in his heat.

My knees part and sink beside his hips, my skin flush as I fold into the trembling press of him.

I make a small sound I don't mean to.

It shatters something inside him. He groans, low and choked, forehead pressed into mine as he fights to steady his breath. "Jesus," he whispers, voice rough as gravel and silk all at once.

I laugh breathlessly, the sound dissolves into another kiss.

My hands explore him like a map I'm memorizing with my fingertips – over the hard plans of his chest, along the ridges of his ribs, down to the taut curve of his abdomen, feeling every pulse beneath the damp warmth of his skin. His breaths hitch under my palms.

Sliding one hand into the waistband of his boxers, I wrap my fingers around him. He responds by trailing that same hungry mouth down my neck, to my collarbone, pausing just an inch from my lips – savoring it all.

He kisses me again, deliberate and slow, as if engraving my taste into his memory. I clutch at his hair, heart pounding, thumb brushing over the droplet of precum at his crown and drawing it along his length.

The air quivers with our ragged breaths, the bed creaks beneath us, and every suppressed moan cuts the hush like fire.

"This stays between us," I murmur, voice thick with need.

He nods, jaw working. "Always."

I can't help the giggle that bubbles up as he grips my hips and lifts, sending me onto the mattress with a delicious thud. He's on me again before thought can catch up to my sensation. His lips descend on mine, then wander lower, mapping the curve of my throat.

He slides the strap of my cami off one shoulder, then the other, and my breasts spill free. He teases one nipple between thumb and forefinger, while his mouth devours the other, teeth grazing lightly until I arch and press into him, burning for friction.

He takes the que and peels my shorts down my legs, then lowers himself so his breath fans across my wetness.

"Hank – " I whimper, clutching his hair as his tongue plunges along my slit, filling me with shockwaves. He pulls back only to dive in again, flicking precise, torturous circles around my clit.

"Such a fucking tease, Lenni," he groans around me. His voice rattles my bones.

He parts my thighs and rises to his knees, the head of him poised at my entrance. He looks down, eyes dark with hunger and something tender.

"Lenni..." he rasps, the question trembling.

"Yes, Hank, fuck me," I cry, part pleading, part command, aching for him to sink into me.

He slides in one torrid inch at a time, stretching me gloriously until he's buried to the hilt. Everything inside me clenches around him in a riot of bliss.

"You feel incredible." He groans, leaning forward to press his chest against mine.

"Don't stop," I gasp, wrapping my legs around his hips. I pull him deeper, wrenching a guttural moan from his throat as he hits every nerve, every secret place no one else could ever touched.

I'm lost in the thrust of him, the primal rhythm he sets, my body trembling with every growl he rolls into me.

"Come for me, baby." He whispers in my ear, voice nearly swallowed by the pounding of our hearts.

And then I shatter – contracting around him, my vision blurs, light explodes behind my eyes as my orgasm rips through me. His follows, his thrusts convulsing, and I feel him pulse deep inside as he comes, our release a singular, blistering triumph.

We collapse together, chest to chest, breath mingling in the soft aftershock of everything we've unleashed.

The quiet realization that nothing has exploded—even though it feels like it should have.

We're tangled together on the bed, chest to

chest, his heartbeat thudding against mine like it's trying to convince itself this is real.

My limbs feel loose and boneless, my skin oversensitive, every nerve still humming from what we just did.

Hank moves before I do.

He disappears into the bathroom and comes back with a towel, warm and soft. I blink at him, still floating somewhere between sensation and reality.

"What are you doing?" I ask, my voice rough.

"The bare minimum." He says simply.

Like it's obvious.

Like care isn't something earned — just something given.

He moves slowly, deliberately, cleaning me with quiet precision. No urgency now, no hunger — just steady hands making sure I'm comfortable, grounded, safe.

Like he assumes this is what happens after. Like he assumes I expect to be taken care of.

And that's the part that catches me off guard.

Because I don't know what to do with a man who treats tenderness like instinct instead of reward.

Something tight inside my chest loosens anyway.

He finishes, sets the towel aside carefully — not tossed, not rushed — then starts to pull away.

I catch his wrist.

"Stay."

The word slips out softer than I intend. More honest.

He stills. "It's risky," he says quietly.

"The door's locked," I tell him. "Everyone thinks I'm asleep."

He searches my face — looking for doubt, regret, fear.

He doesn't find it.

"You're not leaving me," I say, calm and certain.

He exhales slowly, surrendering to something he's been fighting since the moment I touched him.

Then—carefully—he lies beside me.

He doesn't pull me close at first. He gives me the choice.

So I make it.

I curl into him, my head finding the hollow of his shoulder like it belongs there. His arm comes around me instinctively, hand resting warm and steady at my back.

We don't speak.

Outside, the house settles. Laughter fades. Music drifts farther away. The world keeps turning without asking anything from us.

For tonight, that's enough.

I close my eyes, safe against him, one thought settling deep and undeniable:

This wasn't a mistake.

This was a decision.

And he stayed.

CHAPTER 20
Harlan

Virginia

I slid out before the light changed.

The house is quiet in that deep, early way where even the walls seem asleep. Stillness that only exists after something scared happened and nobody knows how to talk about it.

The door closes softly behind me, and I stand there longer than necessary, letting the air hit my skin like I need proof I'm still thinking clearly.

The ocean is gray, calm, indifferent.

Malibu looks like nothing ever happened here.

Like it didn't witness the moment I stopped being just her security and started being something else entirely.

I walk farther than I need to, boots sinking into damp sand, breath slow and measured.

Distance is supposed to reset things.

It doesn't.

Rehearsal that morning moves forward like a machine that doesn't care about what broke or changed overnight.

No one mentions anything.

No one looks too closely.

Lenni steps onto the stage like she always does — fierce, controlled, untouchable beneath the lights.

But now I know what she sounds like when she breathes against my neck.

And that knowledge sits under my ribs like contraband.

The band kills both shows that weekend.

Crowds roar.

Lights burn.

Everything runs exactly as it should.

Except nothing feels the same.

Colby finally gets the message.

He doesn't disappear, he just recalibrates. Keeps his distance. Stops testing boundaries. Drops the casual proximity like he suddenly remembers there are consequences.

That alone tells me everything.

Lenni, on the other hand, does the opposite. She doesn't say anything. She just… reaches.

She finds reasons.

A hand on my bicep when she passes, fingers lingering half a second longer than necessary.

A shoulder brushing mine when there's space to avoid it.

Her knee bumping mine on the bus like an accident that happens too often to be coincidence.

Small touches and quiet confirmations.

Like she's making sure I don't think she regrets what happened.

I don't pull away, but I don't lean in either.

I stay steady. Professional.

Because every time she touches me, I have to remind myself that wanting something doesn't make it safe for her.

I can survive headlines, she can't survive the wrong narrative at the wrong moment.

We don't cross that line again in Malibu.

Not because we don't want to.

Because we're watched.

Because exhaustion replaces courage.

Because privacy disappears the moment we step back onto the bus.

Arizona comes fast, then Nevada.

The miles blur together — short treks, long nights, cards slapped against tabletops, laughter that sounds earned but fragile.

Someone writes lyrics on a napkin.

Grits claims every lap like a monarch surveying his kingdom.

The rhythm of the road returns.

But underneath it, something hums differently now — a tension that isn't new but finally acknowledged.

Vegas is chaos wrapped in neon.

Which means I stay sharper.

More aware.

More controlled.

But the thing that hits me isn't the city.

It's the phone call.

My manager's voice is tight – professional in that way that means the decision already happened and I'm just not being informed.

"Someone got a photo," he says.

Malibu. The beach. Her on my back. Just the two of us.

I close my eyes.

Not because I'm surprised.

Because I know exactly which moment they caught—the one second I stopped scanning. The one second I forgot to look over my shoulder.

The one second the world shrank to sun, salt, and her laugh against my ear.

"The tabs are buzzing," he continues. "Evie is pissed."

That part doesn't rattle me. Evie is always pissed when something escapes her control.

What lands harder is the next line.

"We're pulling you. Ride back to Tennessee. Then you're catching a flight home. You're on leave."

Leave.

The word settles in my chest like a bruise.

The bus feels different after that.

Like everyone knows something broke but no one wants to be the one who names it out loud.

No jokes. No side comments. No casual noise to soften the edges.

Just the low hum of tires and the weight of something ending before anyone agreed to it.

Lenni disappears into her room with Grits more than once. Door shut. Music turned low, like she's trying not to be noticed—even by herself.

She doesn't come find me, and I don't go looking.

Because the moment I see her face, I might choose wrong. So I do what I've always done when something I care about is at risk.

I wide the perimeter, I watch more, speak, less, and make myself smaller.

The trek back to Tennessee feels longer than any distance we've travelled before. Not because of miles. Because every hour feels like a countdown neither of us acknowledges.

When we finally arrive in Tennessee, it's late enough that the world feels suspended between breaths.

I take my time gathering my bag, moving slower than necessary, aware that every second I delay makes leaving feel less real. Outside, the air carries that familiar southern weight — warm but restless — and stepping onto the gravel feels like crossing a line I can't uncross.

The bus door hisses shut behind me.

And then she's there.

No drama. No storm. Just steady presence — composed in that careful way she uses when the world presses too hard against her edges. Grits sits at her side, watching me with alert eyes as if he understands this moment matters more than anyone is willing to say out loud.

She stops a few feet away, close enough that the space between us hums, far enough that we could pretend this is just another goodbye between coworkers.

For a long second, neither of us speaks.

The silence stretches — not awkward, just fragile.

Then she steps forward first.

Her arms wrap around me in what should be a quick, friendly hug — something casual, something safe. Except she doesn't let go right away. Her breath catches against my chest, and her fingers curl into the fabric of my shirt.

The shift is subtle but undeniable.

This isn't casual anymore.

I feel the moment she realizes it too — the slight tension in her shoulders, the way she begins to pull back before stopping halfway, as if letting go requires more strength than she has right now.

So I don't move.

I don't tighten my arms. I don't pull away. I just hold steady and let her decide when the moment ends.

Maybe I need the extra second as much as she does.

When she finally steps back, her gaze lingers

somewhere near my collarbone instead of meeting my eyes. It's safer there, less dangerous than acknowledging everything sitting between us.

"Please keep in touch," she says quietly, her voice softer than I've ever heard it. "This isn't the end."

The words carry hope wrapped carefully in certainty — like she's trying to convince herself as much as me.

I swallow hard, because I don't know if that's true.

And she knows I don't know.

"When they find nothing solid," she continues, lifting her chin slightly, rebuilding composure piece by piece, "you'll be back."

Hope disguised as logic.

I nod, because speaking feels too risky. My voice would betray something I'm not ready to expose — not here, not now.

Her eyes finally lift to mine.

For just a second, the mask slips.

I see the question she won't ask.

Are you going to disappear like everyone else?

The thought hits harder than anything she could say out loud.

I want to promise something — anything — but promises feel reckless when the ground beneath us isn't stable yet. So instead, I hold her gaze long enough that she knows I'm not leaving lightly.

She nods once, as if accepting the answer I

didn't give.

Then she turns.

No hesitation. No looking back.

Grits falls into step beside her as she walks toward the building, her shoulders straight, her pace steady — controlled in that way she uses when she refuses to let anyone see where the cracks are forming.

I stay where I am longer than necessary, watching until the door closes behind her.

Only then does it hit.

The sharp, hollow pull in my chest.

I tell myself this is what protecting her looks like — distance, silence, patience — the things that keep her safe even when they feel like loss.

But the truth settles anyway.

Leaving her doesn't feel like walking away from a job.

It feels like tearing something loose that I didn't realize had already rooted itself inside me.

I watch the ground pull away through a scratched window and don't feel relief—just distance. Measured, deliberate distance. The kind you convince yourself is necessary.

Virginia greets me with gray skies and a quiet

that feels too big for my apartment. I unlock the door, step inside, and let it shut behind me with a soft click that sounds final.

First thing I do is laundry.

It's automatic. Muscle memory. Clothes into piles. Tour dust and salt air and sweat tumbling away in the washer like I can rinse Malibu out of myself if I try hard enough. I unpack. Fold. Dust the shelves that never get dusty because I'm never here long enough for them to need it.

I vacuum lines into the carpet and stand there staring at them like they might tell me something.

They don't. My mind does, though. Loud and relentless.

The photo. The angle. The distance.
The timing.

Someone breached. Or someone had been watching longer than I realized. A lens where there shouldn't have been one. A moment I let myself forget the rules.

That could've cost her everything.

Worse—it could've cost her her life.

The thought sits heavy in my chest, ugly and unforgiving. I replay the beach over and over, searching for the blind spot. The second I relaxed. The second I let myself believe quiet meant safe.

I call my mom because if I don't, I'll spiral.

She answers on the second ring like she always does. "Harlan?"

"I'm home," I say.

She hears the rest anyway.

"The tabloids are spinning things," I add. "Photos. Headlines."

She hums softly, the sound she makes when she's thinking. "I saw them."

I close my eyes. "I'm sorry."

"For what?" she asks gently.

"For dragging noise into your life."

She scoffs. "Honey, noise finds me just fine on its own." Then she pauses. "You know what I saw?"

I wait.

"I saw a light in you," she says. "One I haven't seen in a long time. Maybe ever."

My throat tightens. "Mom—"

"I'm serious," she continues. "You looked… alive. Not on guard. Not braced."

I sit down on the edge of the bed, elbows on my knees. "I care about her," I admit quietly. "But she has a future. A career. A reputation. I can't be the thing that complicates that."

There's silence on the line—thick, understanding.

"You don't get to decide what she deserves all by yourself," my mom says finally. "But I know why you're trying."

We hang up not long after. I sit there with the phone in my hand until the screen goes dark, the silence in my apartment swelling, my chest feels tight.

A week passes.

Seven full days without an assignment.

I don't think that's ever happened.

At first I tell myself it's a break. A rest. A chance to get my head right.

By day two, it feels like punishment.

I run in the mornings until my lungs burn and my legs go heavy, like pain can outrun memory. I come home, shower, scrub at my skin like salt and sunscreen might still be on me. I clean at night—baseboards, counters, corners that don't need attention—because the act of making things orderly is the only way I know to keep from falling apart.

I sleep too much and not enough.

I don't drink, I don't distract, I don't even turn the TV on. I let the quiet do what it wants. And what it wants is her.

Lenni texts here and there. A stupid inside joke that makes my mouth twitch before it drops again. A picture of Grits sprawled across her bed. A video memo of him snoring so loud it's almost funny.

Every text is a doorway I don't let myself walk through.

She's hopeful. Mentions the next leg. The Northeast. Casual, like she's testing the idea without asking it outright.

I stare at the messages longer than I should. I type, delete, type again, delete again.

My thumb hovers over her contact until I open

it without thinking.

Her name fills the screen.

My chest tightens.

Before I can stop myself I press call.

It rings once.

Panic spikes – I end the call before it connects.

I want to tell her I miss her so much it feels like a bruise under my ribs. I want to tell her the apartment smells like nothing and I hate it because the tour smelled like coffee and shampoo and her skin after the sun. I want to tell her that I keep expecting to hear her bare feet in a hallway, her voice calling my name like it's something she owns.

Instead I send something safe. Neutral. A joke. A thumbs up.

Anything that doesn't confess what I'm carrying.

The email comes the next day.

New contract. Start Monday.

Different detail. Different risk. Same rules. I read it once. Then again. Then close the laptop.

This is the job, the life, the part where I disappear and she keeps shining.

I don't tell Lenni I won't be on her next run.

I don't tell her because she deserves the life she's building—the rooms full of people singing her words back to her, the bright momentum, the reputation she fought tooth and nail for.

And because if I tell her the truth, she might ask me to stay anyway. And I don't trust myself to say no twice.

I lie back on my bed, stare at the ceiling, and finally let myself feel it. My chest aches like something essential got cut out and left a hollow behind.

I think about Malibu.

The private stretch of sand. The way she looked at me like she wasn't afraid of what she wanted. The way she pulled me into her room like she was done pretending she could do everything alone.

The way she said *you're not leaving me* like it was fact.

I was supposed to be the steady one.

So why does it feel like she's the only thing that ever made me stop bracing for impact?

I queue up *Broken* – Seether and Amy Lee – and the first note hits like a hand closing around my throat.

I let it play loud enough to drown out my better judgment.

Just for a little while, I let myself be the man I don't get to be on the job.

A man who misses someone.

A man who wants what he shouldn't.

A man who's still tasting the salt of her skin in his memory like it's punishment and prayer at the same time.

I let the song crack me open.

For the quiet beach.

For the line I didn't cross again.

For the woman who trusted me with softness—
and the man I became because of it.

Tomorrow, I'll be steady again.

Tonight, I lie here with the music swallowing the room, and I let the truth have its turn:

I didn't just leave Malibu.

I left her.

And the worst part is—
I'd do it again if it kept her safe.

Even if it ruins me.

CHAPTER 21
Lennon

Tennessee

Home was supposed to feel like landing.
Like relief.
Like I could finally take the weight off and breathe in familiar air without having to scan every room for exits and angles and strangers with phones.

Instead, the second my boots hit the ground, Evie was there—eyes sharp, jaw set, moving like a storm with a clipboard.

"Come on," she had said, already steering me like I was late for my own life. "We need to get ahead of this."

I barely got a word out before she got me in the car, door shut, the world sealed off behind tinted glass. Her phone in her hand, scrolling, tapping, firing off messages like bullets.

"You have *no idea* what you have to lose," she said, voice tight enough to tremble. "Over dating —" she cuts her eyes toward me, expression turning sharp— "the help."

The words hit like ice water.

My stomach twisted. "Don't call him that."

Evie laughed, sharp and humorless. "I'm not insulting him, I'm telling you how they'll frame it. They don't care who he is, Len. They care what it sells."

I stared out the window and watched Tennessee blur past. My hands curled into fists in my lap.

"He's not—" I started.

"He's not what?" she shot back. "A risk? A headline? A liability? Because he is. Whether you meant it to be or not."

She exhaled hard, visibly reining herself in.

"You have an image to uphold," she continued, slower now. "You have a brand. You have contracts. Sponsors. A tour. Staff. People whose mortgages depend on you showing up and not becoming the internet's newest feeding frenzy."

My throat burned. "I didn't do anything wrong."

"That's adorable," Evie said softly — and somehow that softness cut deeper than the anger. "Wrong isn't the point. Perception is."

She swiped her phone again, shoved it closer to my face. A headline. A grainy photo. Me on a back I recognized without seeing his face. A beach that was supposed to be empty.

A moment that was ours.

Stolen.

Evie lowered the phone. "You are gambling everything you've built with a man you can't even be seen with."

"I'm not gambling," I whispered. "I'm living."

Evie looked at me for a long beat, and for a second I saw it—the fear under the anger. The way she wasn't just furious for me, but *terrified* for what would happen when the machine decided to chew.

"Keep the tabloids on Colby," she said finally, shifting strategies. "If they need a story, give them one that costs you nothing. He's been circling you all tour. Let them write *that* narrative. Let them speculate about him. Let them chase him. Not Harlan."

My stomach flipped at the way she said his name like it was combustible.

I didn't argue.

Not because I agreed.

Because I was tired to fight.

By the time we reached my condo, I felt scraped raw.

Ro was there without asking, like she could see the cracks starting to show.

She kicked her shoes off and followed me straight into the kitchen.

"You gonna tell me?" she asked, arms folded, voice gentle but direct.

I poured a glass of water and drank like it'd drown the shaking in my hands.

Then I told her.

Not the bedroom. Not the way his mouth felt against my skin.

Not the things that still felt too sacred to name.

But enough.

The beach.

The way he looked at me. The way he stayed. The way he left like it cost him something.

Ro listened quietly. Her jaw tightened when I repeated Evie's words. Softened at mine.

When I finished, she was quiet for a long moment. Then she said, "I could tell."

I blinked. "You could?"

Ro rolled her eyes like I'm naive.

"Lenni. You look at him like you're starving and he's food."

Heat climbed my neck. "Ro."

"I'm not judging you," she said, stepping closer. "I'm saying you deserve something real. Not whatever glossy, polished version of happiness they're trying to sell with your face on it."

My voice cracked. "I don't know what real looks like right now."

"It looks like you not letting them turn you into a statue," she said softly.

After Ro left, the condo fell quiet.

Not peaceful quiet.

Lonely quiet.

Making me feel every missing thing.

I kept in touch with Hank anyway.

A few texts here and there. Small. Careful. Inside jokes, a picture he sent of a coffee cup, a reply from me with Grits' head in my lap, his eyes half closed.

I missed him so much it startled me.

I'd never had someone feel so much like home.

Not the house kind.
The body kind.
The *I can exhale and stop performing* kind.
Safety.
Steady hands.
A quiet presence that made the world feel less sharp.

Evie said he'd be back for the Northeast trek.
Like she was tossing me a bone.
Like I could earn him again if I behaved.
I nodded like I believed her.
I didn't know if he was coming back to me — or just coming back for the job.

Every time my phone buzzed, my chest tightened. Every time it didn't, it tightened more.
I told myself not to need him.
Told myself I've survived worse than missing a man.
But this wasn't just missing.
This was waiting.
And I've never been good at waiting for things that matter.

The last night before the last run—I don't sleep.
I stretch out on the couch with Grits curled

against my legs and turn the radio up too loud. Loud enough to shake the glass. Loud enough to drown out the ache that's been pacing circles in my chest all week.

Only When It's You by Bleeding Verse comes on and hits me straight in the chest—raw and loud and desperate in a way that feels too honest to survive.

I let it.

I hope I'm annoying the goon squad Evie posted outside my condo.

I hope the bass rattles their teeth.

I hope they hear every lyric and roll their eyes and think, *Here we go again.*

I close my eyes and let the sound swallow me whole.

For three minutes and forty-two seconds, I almost forget what it feels like to miss him.

Then the song ends.

Silence crashes in.

I open my eyes.

And my blood turns to ice.

here's a dark silhouette at my patio door.

Standing still.

Watching me through the glass.

Not moving.

Not leaving.

Just—watching.

Grits' head lifts slowly. A low rumble rolls through his chest, deep and warning.

I don't breathe.

I don't blink.

Because I know this feeling.

The moment when your body recognizes danger before your mind catches up — when instinct whispers, *you've been seen.*

The shape doesn't move.

Just stands there.

Close enough that I can see the outline of shoulders.

The tilt of a head.

Close enough that I know he can see me.

And for one horrible, suspended second, I can't tell if the man in the dark is here to hurt me —

Or if my heart is about to shatter because it isn't the man I've been waiting for.

Because part of me — traitorous and aching — still expects Hank to be the one standing guard when I look up.

My body snaps out of the freeze like a wire's been yanked.

I fumble for the remote, hands clumsy, and slam the music off so hard I almost drop it. The silence is worse. Now I can hear my pulse slamming against my ribs.

I swallow.

Then I scream.

"SECURITY!"

My voice cracks on the second syllable — sharp, ugly, nothing like control.

I don't care.

"SECURITY — NOW!"

Grits is on his feet in an instant, hackles up, a snarl ripping out of him that vibrates through the room.

The silhouette doesn't move.

Not even a flinch.

Like he knew exactly how long he could stand there before someone came.

Like he's waiting.

Like he likes this.

Footsteps thunder down the hall outside my unit. Keys jangle. A radio crackles.

The door bursts open and two men flood inside, scanning corners, clearing sightlines.

"Ma'am — where?"

I point at the patio, arm shaking. "There."

They move fast. One rips the curtain back. The other throws the door open with his body angled in front of me.

Cold night air rushes in.

The balcony is empty.

No shadow.

No figure.

Just the faint sway of the outdoor chair.

Gone.

The absence feels louder than his presence — like he left on purpose, like the point was never getting caught.

One guard swears under his breath and moves left. The other checks right, scanning railings, edges, the drop below.

Nothing.

I step forward without meaning to, barefoot on cold tile.

"How—" My voice comes out thin. "How did he get up here?"

The guard's jaw tightens. "We don't know yet."

A sharp laugh tears out of me. "That's not comforting."

One of the guards steps back inside from the balcony, expression different now.

Tighter.

"There's something out here," he says.

My spine locks.

"What."

He doesn't answer right away. He crouches near the corner of the balcony — near the chair that had been swaying — and reaches down carefully.

Like he's handling evidence.

My stomach drops before he even stands.

It's a folded piece of paper.

Placed where I would see it.

Not random. Not rushed. Intentional — like a conversation waiting for me to answer.

"Don't touch it," I breathe, even though he's already holding it by the edges.

"I won't," he says. "Ma'am… you might not want to read this."

That makes it worse.

"I do."

He hesitates.

Then he unfolds it.

Even from a few feet away, I can see the handwriting.

Blocky.

Pressed hard into the paper.

Like whoever wrote it wanted to carve the words in.

The guard swallows.

Then reads it aloud.

"He can't watch you forever."

The room goes silent.

The air thins.

My heart starts pounding so hard it feels like it's trying to bruise its way out of my chest.

There's one last line.

Written smaller.

More precise.

"Let's see how you sing without him."

Not just a threat — a promise that he's been paying attention to what Hank means to me.

Something inside me snaps.

Not fear.

Not yet.

Fury.

Cold. Controlled. Lethal.

My hands stop shaking.

Because now this isn't just about privacy.

Or tabloids.

Or perception.

This is about someone trying to use the one person who made me feel steady—

As a weapon.

"You need to call the police," the guard says carefully. "And we need to escalate building security immediately."

I nod.

He's already on his radio — camera feeds, blind spots, roof access, stairwells.

It all sounds efficient.

Professional.

Controlled.

It doesn't change the fact that someone stood outside my home and watched me like I was content.

Like I was something to consume.

My hands start to shake.

Not from fear.

From rage.

My body.

My work.

My privacy.

My reputation.

And now—

My home.

My safety.

I turn away from the glass like it's contaminated and grab my phone with fingers that barely work.

I don't think.

I dial.

Evie answers on the first ring. "What."

"There was someone on my patio," I say, words

clipped and fast. "A man. Watching me. Your guys ran in and he was gone before they hit the door."

Silence.

Then, tight: "Are you okay?"

"No," I snap. "I'm not okay, Evie. He got to my patio."

"That's impossible," she fires back instantly. "You're in a secured building. You have two men outside your—"

"He was there," I cut in. "Staring at me."

My chest heaves. I force air into lungs that don't want to cooperate.

"And I'm going to say this once," I add, fury breaking through the cracks, "Hank would've never let this happen."

The line goes quiet.

Too quiet.

"Lenni—"

"No." My voice shakes now, but I don't care. "You pulled him. And the first week he's gone, someone is on my patio. So fix it. Fix it now."

I can hear the pivot on her end — fear turning into command.

"Okay. I'm making calls. Stay inside. Lock everything."

"I am inside," I whisper.

My voice breaks anyway.

"That's the problem."

When I hang up, the condo feels smaller.

Too many windows.

Too much glass.

Too much exposure.

One of the guards is talking about reviewing footage. Another mentions possible access from the neighboring unit's balcony.

All I hear is the truth pounding in my head:

I am not safe in my own life.

Not on stage.

Not off stage.

Not even on my couch.

Grits presses against my leg, tail low, eyes fixed on the patio door like he expects the dark to move again.

I sink down and pull him close, burying my hands in his fur.

Helplessness is a different kind of terror.

It isn't the fear of being hurt.

It's the fear of knowing you can't stop it.

My reflection stares back at me in the glass — layered over black night.

And a brutal, undeniable truth rises through the adrenaline:

Hank wasn't just security.

He was the only thing that made the danger feel containable.

And without him—

The world is already proving how easily it can get in.

CHAPTER 22

Lennon

Pennsylvania

I slept the whole way to New York.

Not the kind of sleep that restores you — the kind that happens when your body finally collapses under the weight of too much adrenaline. Every time I surfaced, it was to the same low murmur of radios outside my door, the quiet shift of boots in the hallway, the steady reminder that I'm never really alone anymore.

Security had doubled overnight.

Maybe tripled.

Like numbers could fix what had already been broken.

There's a new personal guard assigned to me now. He introduced himself when I boarded the bus, voice firm, posture stiff, eyes alert in a way that feels almost rehearsed. I nodded, thanked him, and immediately forgot his name.

Not because I'm ungrateful.

Because he isn't Hank.

He stands too rigid. Watches too obviously. Hovers instead of blending. His presence doesn't expand the room — it shrinks it. I feel managed, escorted, contained.

Hank never felt like containment.

He felt like space.

When we roll into Manhattan, the skyline rises sharp and gray against a cold sky, and my chest feels bruised from the inside out. The bus door hisses open, and the city greets us with flashing cameras, crew chatter, and that constant hum of motion that never quite stops.

I step down.

And I scan.

I don't mean to. It's instinct now — automatic and traitorous.

I already know what I won't find.

Still, my eyes search the perimeter, tracing faces, shoulders, stances.

Hank isn't there.

There's no familiar silhouette holding the edge of the chaos steady. No quiet presence anchoring my left side like a promise. No subtle shift of weight that tells me he's already clocked every exit and every threat before I even think to look.

Just strangers in the same uniform.

And the absence hits harder than the cameras ever could.

The note replays in my head, its words etched deeper now that I'm standing here without him.

My stomach drops so suddenly I have to steady my breath before I take another step. It feels like something inside my ribcage has been removed and left exposed, raw to the air.

Crushed doesn't cover it.

There's something more invasive about this

feeling — like vulnerability has been weaponized.

I swallow down the ugly, irrational flicker of betrayal that tries to rise. I know he didn't choose to leave. I know this was logistics and strategy and management.

But logic doesn't speak the same language as my heart.

My heart only knows that someone stood outside my home and watched me — and Hank wasn't there.

I walk into the venue like I'm not unraveling.

I smile at fans pressed against barricades. I wave. I sign whatever they hand me. My voice stays steady when I thank them for coming. My hands don't tremble.

Armor is muscle memory.

Inside, the atmosphere shifts. Conversations lower. Security briefings happen in tight clusters. Words drift through the air — roof access, neighboring unit, blind spots, footage review.

I sit in my dressing room while someone checks the hinges on the door. Another person tests the locks. There's a conversation about adjusting my exit routes after the show. Someone mentions rerouting the bus parking.

It's all efficient.

Professional.

Necessary.

It still doesn't change the fact that someone stood outside my glass door and watched me like

I was part of the set.

And the sickest part is this: the note wasn't just a threat. It was psychological precision.

It wasn't about getting close.

It was about proving Hank wasn't here.

The stalker didn't just want access to my space.

He wanted access to my stability.

Let's see how you sing without him.

I refused to cancel tonight.

Not because I feel brave.

Because canceling would mean admitting I'm not okay, and I don't know how to be not okay in public without becoming something people consume. A spectacle. A breakdown. A trending topic.

So I sit still while makeup is applied. I let them zip me into leather. I let glitter catch the light across my collarbones like armor forged in sequins.

The new guard stands outside my door like a replacement part.

Present.

Capable.

Wrong.

And in the quiet space before call time, when the noise of the city fades and the reality of what happened settles into my bones, one truth rises with devastating clarity.

I love him.

Not a crush.

Not a headline.

Not a convenient tour attachment.

Love.

The kind that rearranges your sense of safety.

The kind that makes you furious someone tried to use it against you.

The kind that makes you understand exactly how exposed you are without it.

For the first time since this all started, the fear shifts.

It isn't just about me.

If someone knows enough to taunt me about Hank...

If someone knows he was here and that he's gone...

Then they know enough to look for him.

And the thought of danger turning in his direction —

That's the thing that truly makes my pulse spike.

Because I can survive being hunted.

I don't know if I can survive something happening to him.

The next show was Pennsylvania.

The entire day, my phone lived in my hand

like a pulse I was afraid to lose. I told myself I wouldn't spiral. I told myself Hank was probably busy, probably on assignment, probably somewhere without service.

I texted him anyway.

Something light. Something that didn't sound like panic.

You okay?

I stared at the screen longer than I should have.

Then another.

Where are you?

The typing bubble never appeared.

By mid-afternoon, the fear had shifted from irritation to something colder.

Please.

That one sat there the longest. Vulnerable. Bare.

No response.

I called.

Straight to voicemail.

I hung up and called again, because sometimes technology lies and sometimes hope is stubborn.

Voicemail.

By the time I was in hair and makeup, my chest hurt in a way that felt structural, like something inside me was splintering under pressure.

I stared at myself in the mirror while Tess perfected my eyeliner. My lips were painted into confidence. My hair was styled into effortless control. I looked exactly like the version of me the world expected.

But none of it mattered if I couldn't find the one person who made me feel like I could breathe without effort.

I walked onto that stage anyway.

I sang like my heart wasn't breaking in real time.

I smiled like my world wasn't cracking at the seams.

The crowd roared. Lights flashed. Lyrics poured out of me with muscle memory precision.

But every time I glanced toward the wings, some irrational part of me expected to see him there. Steady. Watching. Present.

Every time I didn't, something inside me sank further.

After the show, when the adrenaline drained and the applause faded, I sat alone in my dressing room and stared at my phone like I could will it to light up.

It didn't.

So I did the thing I never do.

I called my mom.

She answered on the first ring, her voice warm and soft like she'd been holding space for me without knowing it. "Baby?"

My voice cracked on the first word. "Mama."

The word undid me.

"Mama," I breathed, and my voice cracked before I could stop it.

And then everything came out.

The tabloids. The note. The silhouette on my balcony. Evie's sharp-edged warnings. The way it feels like the world keeps taking pieces of me as if I owe it something.

And then him.

Hank.

The beach. The steadiness. The quiet strength of him. The way he left without drama, because that's who he is.

The way he hasn't come back.

"I can't do this without him," I whispered, tears hot and humiliating. "I don't want to."

My mother didn't correct me.

She didn't tell me love makes you reckless. She didn't remind me of contracts or consequences or optics.

She just listened.

And when I finally ran out of air, she said softly, "I'm proud of you."

I swallowed hard. "For what?"

"For surviving," she said. "For building something out of nothing. For showing up even when it costs you."

My throat tightened around the truth of that. "I don't feel strong."

"You don't have to all the time," she replied gently. "Strength isn't pretending you're fine. Sometimes it's knowing when to put something big down so you can pick something more important up."

The sentence landed like permission.

Like my mother — the woman who watched me chase this dream from a porch swing in Virginia — was giving me something I've never allowed myself.

The right to choose.

"I love him," I whispered again, because it felt terrifying and solid all at once.

"I know," she said, without hesitation. "And I'm not afraid of that for you."

When we hung up, I sat still for a long moment. My reflection stared back at me — glittered, polished, powerful.

And finally honest.

I didn't deliberate.

I didn't strategize.

I moved.

I found one of the security guys rotating outside my door — the one who'd mentioned knowing Hank in passing, like it wasn't a thing.

"What's your name?" I asked.

He blinked, surprised. "Drew."

"Drew," I said steadily, "I need Hank's address."

His entire posture stiffened. "Ma'am, I can't—"

"You can," I said quietly, stepping closer. Not aggressive. Certain. "Someone was on my patio in Tennessee. Someone left a note about him. He hasn't answered me all day. Hank is the only person I trust right now. So if you're his friend, you're going to help me."

Conflict flashed across his face.

Then I softened.

"Please," I said. Not a command now. A confession. "I need him."

That broke him.

He pulled out his phone slowly, typed, then turned the screen toward me without handing it over.

An address in Virginia.

My pulse kicked hard enough to make my vision blur.

I didn't hesitate.

I found Evie.

She was already on her phone, juggling logistics like she could reroute the weather itself.

"Set up a private flight," I said.

She didn't look up. "No."

"I'm not asking."

That made her raise her head.

"Lenni—"

"I'm going to Virginia," I said, voice calm in the way it gets when I've crossed a line inside myself. "Tonight."

Evie's expression shifted from irritation to alarm. "You're spiraling."

"I'm making a choice," I corrected. "Do your job."

For a long moment, she just stared at me, running numbers in her head — headlines, fallout, sponsorship risk, tour disruption.

Then she exhaled sharply and started tapping on her phone.

"Fine," she said. "I'll set it up."

When the ride finally pulled up out back, Evie stepped in front of me like she could physically block the decision.

"This is insane," she hissed.

I gave her a humorless smile. "So is calling him 'the help.'"

Her jaw tightened.

I stepped around her.

"Lenni," she snapped, voice rising. "If you do this, you're going to regret it."

I paused long enough to meet her eyes.

"Maybe," I said quietly. "But not as much as I'll regret letting you treat me like a product."

The word landed harder than anything else had.

Her expression flickered—anger, fear, something like wounded control.

In that moment, I understood something clearly:

She's terrified of losing the machine.

I'm terrified of losing the man.

I chose.

I lifted my hand and flicked her off.

I said simply, "You're done."

Evie stared at me like I'd just thrown a match into gasoline.

I didn't look back, because fear is loud, and I finally learned how to turn the volume down.

I walked toward the SUV with my heart pounding and my future cracking open in front of me.

For the first time since the silhouette on my balcony – I didn't feel hunted.

I felt decided.

And I didn't care what the headlines would say.

I only cared about getting to him.

CHAPTER 23
HARLAN

Virginia

I'd just dozed off.

Not real sleep—just that thin, drifting state where your body finally shuts down but your mind keeps one eye open. My duffel sat by the door, packed for a new assignment in the morning. Boots lined up. Phone face-down on the nightstand like if I didn't look at it, it couldn't keep reminding me of everything I was choosing to walk away from.

From her.

Ignoring her messages felt like cutting off pieces of myself one at a time, but it was the only way I knew how to keep her safe. Distance was protection. Distance was discipline.

Distance was the only thing that kept me from ruining her life.

The knock comes late enough to be feel wrong.

I'm upright instantly, instincts snapping into place before thought catches up. My hand moves automatically, scanning for threats, already calculating angles and exits.

No one should be here.

I check the peephole.

And everything inside me stutters.

I open the door anyway.

Lenni doesn't hesitate.

She launches into me – arms wrapping tight, legs locking around my waist, mouth finding mine like she crossed every mile between us just to prove I was real. Her hands frame my face like she's afraid I'll vanish if she lets go.

"I love you, Harlan Godfrey," she breathes against my mouth, voice shaking, fierce and desperate all at once.

I catch her on instinct as the door slams shut behind us. She smells like travel and adrenaline and something raw that reaches straight through my defenses.

It takes everything in me to pull back enough to breathe.

"My name's Hank," I murmur, softer than I mean to.

It's not a correction.

It's an offering.

It undoes her.

Her face crumples, tears spilling fast and sudden, and she collapses against me, arms wrapping tight around my neck like she's holding on in a storm.

"You were supposed to come back for me," she whispers, voice breaking open against my shoulder — not accusation, not anger, just a wound that never learned how to close.

The words hit like something older than us, heavier than this moment — like she's not just talking about now, but every time she learned to stop waiting.

I tighten my hold without thinking, one hand coming up to cradle the back of her head as she trembles against me.

She kisses me again, harder this time, like crying didn't weaken her — it burned away whatever distance I tried to build.

I back us toward the couch without thinking, sitting as she settles into my lap, hands gripping my shirt like it's the only thing keeping her steady.

"I missed you," she whispers, forehead pressed to mine. "God, I missed you."

I brush my thumb under her eye, catching a tear before it falls.

"I'm right here."

The words feel heavier than they should.

Because I wasn't.

Because I chose not to be.

She nods, breath hitching. "He came for me."

Every muscle in my body tightens.

"Who?" I ask, steady but sharp now, hands firm at her waist.

Her eyes fill again. "At my condo. The last night. A man on my patio. Just… standing there. Watching."

Ice floods my veins.

"They didn't tell you?" she asks, disbelief threading through her voice. "They never caught him."

Rage flashes hot and immediate, but I shove it down and pull her closer instead, my grip instinctively protective.

"You're safe now," I say, the promise automatic. Absolute.

"I love you," she whispers again. "I've never felt so safe."

The words hit deeper than anything else she's said.

Because I left.

Because I thought removing myself was protecting her.

"I'm here," I murmur into her hair. "I've got you."

Tomorrow I was supposed to leave for another assignment.

Tonight, that plan feels like something from another life.

My hands move automatically over her shoulders, down her back — not possessive, but checking. Grounding. Making sure she's real, unhurt, here.

"How did you get here?" I ask, pulling back just enough to look at her face. My thumbs frame her jaw, grounding us both.

She explains quickly — private flight, security, Evie. Each detail calms one part of me while another part flares with protective anger that she felt she had to come alone.

"You should've told me," I say quietly.

"I tried," she whispers. "You didn't answer."

The guilt lands heavy.

I close my eyes briefly.

"I was trying to protect you," I admit finally. "If they think you and I are connected — if someone's targeting you — distance keeps you safer."

Her expression softens, but she shakes her head.

"I wasn't chasing danger," she says.

I tilt her chin gently. "Then what were you doing?"

Her gaze locks on mine.

"I was chasing you."

The honesty hits harder than any accusation.

I pull her closer, one arm tight around her back as her heartbeat settles against my chest.

She exhales, the tension easing just a little.

"Good. Now you know how it feels."

Despite everything, a quiet breath of laughter slips out of me.

"You're not going anywhere," she says then — not a question.

My eyes drift toward the duffel by the door.

Toward the life I thought I had to choose instead.

Then back to her.

"No," I say finally. "I'm not."

Relief floods her face, and she leans into me like she's finally allowed to exhale.

"I love you," she says again, quieter now.

I kiss her hair, her temple, her cheek—everywhere but her mouth, because if I start there I won't stop.

"I know," I tell her. "And I'm not letting anything happen to you. Not on my watch. Not ever."

I shift us deeper into the couch, her still straddling me, my arms a barricade around her.

Outside, the world can wait.

Inside, I'm counting exits, threats, possibilities—and one unmovable truth:

She came to me when she was afraid.

And that makes her my responsibility in a way no contract ever could.

"Take me to bed, Hank," she says.

It's not breathless or shy.

It's a demand built out of need.

My resolve doesn't shatter—it *moves*.

I scoop her up without another word, her legs locking around my waist like she's been waiting for this exact second. She buries her face in my neck as I carry her down the short hallway, every step deliberate, grounding myself in the feel of her weight, her warmth, the reality of her being here.

My room is dark except for the soft spill of city light through the blinds.

I lay her down like a man possessed, like worship and hunger are the same prayer.

Like she's not just something to keep – but something I can't survive without.

I kneel and undo her boots, each lace a barrier I can barely stand. Her eyes lock with mine, dark and knowing, her chest already rising and falling in rhythm with my own racing heart.

I peel her socks away, my fingertips burning paths across her skin, my grip on her ankles tightening with barely contained need.

When my hand claims her foot, she gasps – a sound that shoots straight through me.

I devour her inch by inch, my mouth marking territory up her leg, her thigh, my teeth brazing skin as I strip away her shorts and fishnets.

Her head falls back. Her pulse hammering visibly at her throat.

When I return to my bed, I don't just pull her to me – I crush her against my chest, our bodies colliding like we're trying to break through each other's skin. My arms lock around her, possessive, and desperate.

Mine.

My hands rake beneath her cropped tee, branding her neck, and when I snap the clasp at her spine, she moans into my mouth, kissing me like she's trying to steal my breath for herself.

There's no space left between us.

Just fire. Just need. Just the raw, savage truth of two people consuming each other in the dark.

I grip her harder, my fingers shoving the barrier of lace to the side, finding her wet and ready. She cries out, arching against me as I claim her mouth again, my forehead pressed to hers hard enough to anchor us both to earth.

"I've got you," I growl against her lips, the words more threat than comfort.

I drive deeper, harder, adding another finger to her dripping center as she floods my hand, her sounds feral and desperate.

She tears her panties down and I withdraw my fingers only to replace them with my dick. Burying myself inside her in one merciless thrust that makes us both cry out.

Her heat grips me like a vise, better than memory, better than fantasy.

I pound into her relentlessly, thumb circling her clit until she convulses beneath me, her release triggering my own savage climax.

We cling to each other like gravity might fail if we don't. I brace my forehead against hers, my hands firm and steady, holding her here. Holding *us* here.

She's flushed, wrecked, beautiful in that quiet aftermath way that tells me this wasn't just want.

It was need.

I stay with her through it. Through the slowing breath. Through the way her body settles back into itself. I don't rush. I don't pull away.

Because this isn't something I take.

It's something I choose.

I brush my thumb over her cheek, gentle now, grounding us both. Her eyes meet mine—open, vulnerable, unguarded in a way that knocks the air out of my chest.

I don't plan the words.

They just come.

"I love you, Lennon Vale."

The silence that follows is loud.

Her breath catches. Her mouth opens like she's about to say something and can't find the shape of it yet. So she just wraps her arms around me and buries her face in my neck, holding on like I might disappear if she doesn't.

I pull her closer, tucking her against my chest, my body curved around hers like a promise.

Outside, the night keeps moving. Assignments, headlines, danger—none of it matters right now.

I didn't let go.

And I won't.

Not tonight.

Not after this.

Not ever.

CHAPTER 24
LENNON

Virginia

I wake slowly.

Not because something startled me awake. Not because my body is bracing for impact or my mind is already running through schedules and expectations.

I wake because I feel… safe.

Sunlight filters through the blinds in thin golden lines, warming the sheets, touching bare skin, turning everything soft around the edges.

Hank is still asleep.

That alone almost makes me smile.

He's on his back, one arm wrapped loosely around me like even unconscious he doesn't forget where I am. His breathing is deep, steady. Grounded.

I don't move at first.

I just watch him.

The strong lines of his face softened by sleep. The quiet strength that never leaves him — even when he rests. One hand lies open against my back like he trusts I won't disappear.

Something shifts inside my chest.

Not the frantic relief I felt when I first got here. Something steadier.

Something rooted.

I'm not clinging anymore.

I'm choosing.

I slide my fingers slowly along his jaw, tracing the stubble there, memorizing the shape of him. His eyes open almost immediately — instinct, awareness — but when he realizes it's just me, the tension melts.

"Hi," I whisper.

His mouth curves slightly.

"Hi."

The word feels heavier this morning. Fuller.

"Did I dream you?" I ask softly.

"Nope."

Relief hits me before I can stop it. It must show on my face because his expression softens in that quiet way he has — the one that makes me feel seen instead of handled.

"You're still here," I say.

"I said I wasn't going anywhere."

And this time, I believe him.

Not because he promises it.

Because I see the choice behind it.

I kiss him — slow, unhurried, not desperate like last night. Just warm and certain.

We stay tangled together longer than we need to, breathing each other in, letting morning settle around us like something sacred.

Eventually I stretch, rolling onto my back.

"I forgot what it feels like to wake up without an audience," I admit quietly.

The words surprise me even as I say them.

Without cameras. Without expectations. Without needing to perform strength.

He doesn't rush to respond. He just pulls me closer, arm wrapping around me like gravity.

"You don't need armor here," he says.

And something inside me loosens.

Not because he says it.

Because he means it.

My phone buzzes on the nightstand. I grab it lazily, still tucked into his side.

Ro.

Relief floods me as I read.

"They're back home," I say, turning the screen toward him. "Everything's okay. Grits too."

I laugh softly at the photo she sends — Grits sprawled like a king across a couch.

"He looks deeply traumatized," Hank murmurs.

"Absolutely suffering."

I set the phone down and curl back into him without thinking, settling against his warmth like it's the most natural place in the world.

"I didn't realize how much I was holding in," I admit quietly.

His hand moves slowly over my back, steady and grounding — not gripping, not claiming — just there, present, following the rhythm of my breathing until it evens out.

"You don't have to carry it alone anymore."

The words settle deep, but it isn't just the protection in his voice that hits me.

It's the respect.

He isn't trying to rescue me from myself or take control of the weight I carry. He doesn't tighten his hold or pull me closer like I might break. Instead, his palm stays warm and open against my spine, like he trusts me to stand on my own even while he stands beside me.

And somehow that feels stronger than being saved.

Later, the shower becomes warmth and laughter instead of urgency. Steam curls around us, softening everything. He shifts slightly so the water hits my shoulders first, one hand braced lightly against the wall near me — not trapping me, just instinctively placing himself between me and the world even here.

Standing under warm water with him feels… normal.

And the realization surprises me.

I don't want extraordinary every day.

I want this.

Coffee brewing in the background. Quiet mornings. Him.

He cooks while I sit on the counter watching him, stealing bites and pretending I'm not completely undone by how steady he looks moving through his own space. Every so often he glances over his shoulder just long enough to check that I'm still there — not suspicious, just aware — and each time our eyes meet, something warm passes between us.

"This is dangerously domestic," I tease.

"You don't hate it," he says, flipping the eggs without looking, **on**e hip bumping gently against the counter where my knee brushes him — a small, unconscious connection.

"I absolutely do not hate it," I admit, voice dropping playfully. "I'm just trying not to climb you like a tree."

His laugh is quiet but real, shoulders loosening in a way that tells me he's relaxed in a way he rarely allows himself to be.

"You want to meet your biggest fans?" he asks casually, sliding a plate toward me before I even reach for it.

"Oh?"

"My sister," he clarifies. "And my mom."

I blink, the weight of that settling slowly.

"You're serious?"

"I don't joke about my mom," he deadpans, but there's a softness in his eyes when he looks at me – a quiet invitation instead of pressure.

I laugh softly, but underneath it something shifts — nerves, excitement, the understanding that this isn't casual anymore.

Meeting family is real.

"You sure?" I ask quietly. "Because I thought you were my biggest fan."

He steps closer, hands settling at my hips – not pulling, not directing – just anchoring. His thumbs move once, slow and absentminded, like reassurance rather than possession.

"That goes without saying."

My breath catches, warmth spreading through me at the quiet certainty in his voice.

"Well," I say softly, "I guess I should meet the people who raised the man who makes me feel strong enough to be myself."

His gaze changes then — not dark or territorial, just deeply present — like he hears the weight behind the words. His hand shifts slightly, not tightening but steadying, and I realize he isn't seeing someone fragile in front of him.

He sees me.

Strong. Capable. Choosing.

And that realization settles into me.

This isn't temporary.

This isn't reckless.

This is something real. Something steady. Something strong enough to survive whatever comes next.

And for the first time, I don't feel like I'm falling into love.

I feel like I'm walking toward it — choosing him as clearly as he's choosing me.

On the drive, Virginia rolls past in green and

gold blurs. I watch him more than the road, the steady way he drives, the quiet confidence that never demands attention but always earns it.

I pull out my phone and type quickly.

Me: *Find two tickets for the VA show this weekend. Front row. Non-negotiable.*

My thumb hovers for a second before I sent it.
Done.

"What are you smiling about?" he asks without looking at me.

"World domination."

He snorts.

I love that sound more than I should.

His mom's house feels warm before we even step inside. Wind chimes sing softly as we walk up the porch steps, and I feel my nerves creep in unexpectedly.

Hank squeezes my hand — not tight enough to lead me, just firm enough to remind me I'm not walking in alone.

The door opens and suddenly I'm being pulled into laughter and warmth and a family that feels like sunlight instead of scrutiny.

They see us immediately.

And instead of pressure — there's welcome.

Real welcome.

"Oh," she says slowly. "Oh wow."

Heat floods my cheeks.

"Don't start," Hank mutters.

She ignores him completely.

Another woman steps into view behind her—softer, steady, observant. His mom.

And I feel it immediately.

Not judgment. Recognition.

"You must be Lennon," she says gently, stepping forward and taking my hands in a way that feels grounding instead of examining — like she already understands something about me without needing proof.

"Yes ma'am," I say automatically.

She smiles. "None of that. You're family here."

The word hits me harder than I expect.

Lunch becomes laughter before I realize it's happening. Stories about Hank as a kid. His sister teasing him mercilessly. His mom watching us both with a quiet warmth that makes my chest ache.

They see it.

The chemistry. The connection. The way my knee keeps brushing his under the table – and every time it happens, his hand shifts subtly closer, like an unconscious promise.

His sister practically vibrates with excitement.

When it's finally time to leave, I pause by the door and pull out my phone.

"I need your emails," I tell them.

His sister blinks. "Why?"

"Trust me."

They exchange a look but give them anyway.

A second later their phones ding.

His sister opens hers and screams.

"No. No way. LENNI. VALE."

She looks at Hank like he personally arranged this miracle.

"These are front row."

I shrug, suddenly shy. "You're family now."

The words slip out before I can stop them.

And the way Hank looks at me afterward nearly knocks the breath out of me – not surprised, not overwhelmed – proud. Like he already knew I had this kind of heart.

The drive back is comfortably quiet.

I rest my head against his shoulder at a stoplight, tracing slow circles over his arm, grounding myself in the reality of him.

When we walk back into his apartment, I don't let him get far.

I step in front of him.

"I did something," I say.

His brow lifts. "That sounds dangerous."

"I hired you."

He blinks. "You… what?"

"You're officially my personal bodyguard now," I say, lifting my chin slightly. "On my books. My contract."

His expression shifts—surprise, concern, something deeper.

"I'm not doing this without you," I add softly. "Not again."

The room goes quiet.

He steps closer, hands sliding to my waist,

closing the distance slowly.

"You know what that means?" he murmurs, his voice rough with need.

"Yes," I say, pulse thundering in my throat. "It means I choose you."

His eyes ignite – molten gold and midnight black.

He lifts me onto the counter in one fluid motion, my startled gasp dissolving into a desperate kiss that consumes us both.

His mouth brands a scorching patch down my jaw, my neck, setting every nerve ending ablaze. I arch back as he presses me flat against the cold granite, the contrast shocking against my feverish skin.

The world fractures. Reality shatters.

My bottoms vanish beneath his demanding hands. His tongue devours me, relentless and precise, making me writhe and claw at the counter's edge.

His fingers drive deeper, harder, curling inside me until I'm sobbing his name. I grip his hair so tightly I must be hurting him, but he growls – a primal sound that vibrates through my core – and when his teeth graze that perfect spot, I explode into blinding fragments.

Wave after merciless wave crashes through me as he refuses to let me come down.

I'm trembling, begging, pulling him up to me with savage need.

"Hank – God – please – " the words tear from

my throat.

His eyes lock on mine, possessive and raw.

"Your Hank," he growls claiming my mouth with bruising intensity.

I collapse against him, chest heaving, every nerve still humming as he gathers me closer, slower now, careful where moments ago he was relentless.

He brushes a stray hair behind my ear, then his hand slides up my back.

Steady.

Safe.

We stay like that for a while, breath slowly finding rhythm again.

"I love you, Lennon Vale," he murmurs, the words low against my hair.

My throat tightens. Not from shock.

From recognition.

"I know," I whisper back, pressing my face into his neck, inhaling him like oxygen.

Eventually he lifts me into his arms and carries me to his bed. The world feels softer there — quieter — like everything sharp has been dulled by warmth and certainty.

My fingers trace slow lines across his chest, memorizing the steady rise and fall beneath my palm. He covers us with the blankets, tucking me closer in a way that feels like belonging instead of protection.

For the first time, I don't feel hunted or watched or like I'm performing.

I just feel held.

His heartbeat is steady beneath my ear, a rhythm my body recognizes instantly. My breathing slows to match it.

Outside, the night presses against the windows, full of everything waiting for us tomorrow — tour schedules, headlines, decisions we haven't made yet.

But here, none of it matters.

Here, it's just us.

I close my eyes, letting sleep pull me under, safe enough to finally let go.

And as the room fades to darkness, one thought settles deep in my chest:

Whatever comes next — I'm not running from it.

Not anymore.

CHAPTER 25

HARLAN

Virginia

We got a couple domestic mornings tucked away in my apartment. Coffee and quiet music, her bare feet on my hardwood. Her stealing my hoodies and wearing them.

The way I would catch myself watching her. Reading on the couch, laughing at something on her phone, and the way she hummed under her breath when she thought I wasn't listening.

And it hit me every time:

This is what I've been missing.

Not the chaos or the job.

The calm.

The quiet that doesn't feel empty – it feels earned.

But then it's back to work.

The venue. The schedule. The crowd.

We move back into motion like flipping a switch—duffels packed, routes planned, comms checked, threat assessments tightened.

I slide back into security mode the second we pull up, because I don't get to be soft in public.

Not with her.

Not with what's at stake.

And I don't miss the irony:

The thing I'm protecting now isn't just a client.

It's the life she fought to take back.

Backstage is a controlled storm—crew rushing, sound checks, instrument cases rolling, radios chirping. I do my sweeps.

I've got eyes everywhere.

But I still feel the pull—constant—toward the one person in this building who can undo me with a smile.

When the lights drop and the crowd erupts, I take my position off to the side, exactly where I can see the front row and the wings and the access points.

Exactly where I can see her.

Front row is a gut punch. My mom stands there, hands clasped tight, eyes shining. My sister beside her, practically vibrating out of her skin. And next to them—Lenni's mom—quiet, proud, already crying.

Three women. Three different worlds. All of them watching the same girl like she's a miracle.

Lenni comes out and the place loses its mind.

She owns the stage the way she always does—effortless, lethal, luminous.

But there's a steadiness to her tonight that I haven't seen before. Not just confidence. Ownership.

Like she's not just singing.

Like she's choosing.

Halfway through the set, she strips it down.

Porch light performance.

Acoustic.

The band steps back, the spotlight tightens, and she settles onto a stool with her guitar. Legs crossed in a leather mini skirt, a leather tassel vest catching the light when she moves.

She's stunning.

And she's brave.

The crowd quiets. Even security guards stop shifting their weight. Even the air holds still.

She strums, slow and steady, and then she looks out over the sea of people preparing to do something dangerous.

Her voice carries soft at first—then stronger.

"Y'all... I've spent a long time letting other people tell my story."

A ripple moves through the crowd.

"I've spent a long time thinking if I just worked harder, stayed quieter, behaved better—then I'd be safe."

She smiles, but it's not performative. It's honest.

"And I realized something. When you lose sight of what matters most... sometimes you have to fire your manager, piss off the headlines, and take your life back."

The audience erupts—cheers and laughter and applause that feels like support.

My sister's hands fly to her mouth.

My mom is crying now, openly.

Lenni's mom closes her eyes like she's praying.

Lenni looks down at her guitar, then back up, eyes searching—until they find me where I'm standing in the wings.

Her smile changes.

Softens.

Claims.

"That's what I'm here to do tonight," she says, voice steady. "And this... this one is for my Hank."

My lungs forget how to work.

The crowd reacts, a wave of "awww" and cheers, but I don't hear them.

All I hear is her.

She strums again, gentle, familiar.

And then she sings "*When You Say Nothing At All*"—acoustic, stripped down, pure.

Not a performance – a confession dresses as music.

I've done this job a long time. I've stood in a hundred wings and watched a hundred shows. I've been unmoved by screaming crowds and pyrotechnics and staged intimacy.

This breaks me anyway.

The audience is captivated—silence that only happens when people can feel they're witnessing something true.

Lenni finishes the last line and lets the final chord ring out.

Then she looks right at me.

And she makes the decision for both of us.

"Hank," she says into the mic, voice warm and

unshakable. "Come here."

Every head in the venue turns toward the wing.

My body goes rigid, instincts flaring—security protocol screaming that this is a mistake.

And underneath it all, something else rises up: Her.

The way she walked into my apartment and chose me like it was the simplest thing in the world.

I start moving.

Because when she calls me, I go.

I step onto the stage.

The lights hit me. The crowd surges—cheers exploding like they've been waiting for this reveal. I can feel a thousand eyes on my skin, cameras lifting, phones glowing.

Lenni stands from her stool and meets me halfway.

Her hand slides into mine like it's always belonged there.

She lifts our joined hands—high, clear, undeniable.

Her lips find mine and in that moment, with the roar of the crowd and the cameras and the world trying to write its own version of this—
She claims me anyway.

To the world.

To herself.

And I let her.

The roar follows us offstage like heat.

It's still vibrating in the hallway—fans screaming, crew clapping, someone laughing too loud because adrenaline needs somewhere to go.

Lenni is glowing from the spotlight, cheeks flushed, hair a little wild, and for half a second she looks lighter than I've ever seen her.

Then it happens.

We round the corner toward the green room and her whole body goes... blank.

Not tired. Not overwhelmed.

Frozen.

Her hand slips from mine without her noticing. Her eyes lock on something and it's like the color drains out of her face one drop at a time.

Not shock. Recognition. Hitting bone before it hits thought.

"Lenni," I say low. "Eyes on me."

She doesn't blink.

My gaze follows her.

And there's a man — wrong energy, wrong posture, wrong presence.

No lanyard.

No pass.

Too calm.

My blood turns cold.

I shift without thinking, angling my body between her and him, blocking his direct line of sight before anyone else notices the change.

Every instinct I have goes razor sharp. The world narrows into angles and exits and distance calculations.

"Control, I've got an unidentified male..." I say, voice clipped, controlled. "No credentials. In the restricted corridor off stage left. Mid-forties, average build, dark jacket — moving toward the service hall."

My team responds instantly in my ear.

I shift my body slightly, putting myself between Lenni and his line of sight. I don't touch her yet—touch can break someone the wrong way when they're frozen.

Her breathing is shallow. Too shallow. She looks like she's holding herself together by will alone.

"Stay with her," I tell the nearest guard, low and firm. "Do not leave her."

He nods, moving in. "Ma'am, this way."

Lenni still looks like she can't hear anything.

The man changes direction.

Not fast enough.

I take off.

He clocks me the moment I move. His shoulders tense. His pace quickens.

"Subject is running," I snap into my comm. "Heading toward the loading corridor. Cut him off."

He makes it ten steps.

I make it eight.

When I hit him, it's not anger.

It's procedure.

It's instinct.

It's the part of me that doesn't hesitate when something threatens what I protect.

But underneath it – rage coils tight and hot, waiting for permission.

I slam into him shoulder-first and drive him into the wall. He grunts, tries to twist away, but I pin him with my forearm and the weight of my body.

"Credentials," I growl. "Now."

He fumbles, hands shaking, digging into pockets like he expects a miracle to appear.

Nothing.

I wrench his arms behind him and lock them down. "You don't have a pass," I say, voice low and lethal. "You don't belong back here. Who are you?"

He spits a laugh that's all wrong. "Does it matter?"

Yes.

It matters more than he knows.

I drag him — literally drag him — down the corridor toward the security office. He stumbles, heels scraping tile, but adrenaline has turned me into something unmovable.

Inside the security office, fluorescent light hums overhead. Monitors glow. Radios crackle.

I shove him into a chair.

"Lock it down," I order. "Nobody in. Nobody out."

A guard cuffs him to the reinforced chair

bracket bolted to the floor.

"Search him." I tell a guard, never taking my eyes off his face.

The man stares up at me with a smugness that makes my skin crawl.

And that's when the door handle rattles.

My head snaps toward the door, "Keep her out."

The guard hesitates.

"Open. The. Door." Lenni's voice cracks through the metal like a whip.

Not hysterical.

Not panicked.

Furious.

And something else.

Certain.

I move toward the door just as it opens.

Lenni stands there, chest rising too fast, eyes burning. Her mom behind her, pale and confused.

"You're not coming in here," I tell her, low and controlled.

Her gaze locks onto mine.

"Move."

There's no plea in it.

No fear.

Just command.

"Lenni—"

"You don't get to decide that for me," she says, voice shaking but unbreakable. "Move."

I see it now. This isn't about safety anymore.

This is about power. And if I block her now, I take that from her.

My jaw tightens.

I step aside. Not because I lose control, but because she takes it.

Her eyes go straight to him.

She's visibly shaking now, but it's no longer paralysis.

It's fury.

Her arms are wrapped tight around herself like she's holding something volatile in place.

Behind her, her mom's face shifts from confusion to dawning horror.

"Why are you in here?" her mom demands. "What is going on?"

Lenni stops three feet from him.

Close enough that he can see her clearly.

Close enough that he knows she's not hiding anymore.

Her chin lifts.

Tears gather — bright, furious — but they don't fall.

Then her voice cuts through the room like shattered glass.

"You," she says, shaking with rage. "It was you all this time. You freak."

The man smiles.

Actually smiles.

It's the kind of expression that makes violence feel righteous.

"Did you miss me, Lennon?" he says smoothly.

Every muscle in my body goes rigid.

Her mom makes a small, confused sound.

Lenni's hands curl into fists.

"You don't get to say my name," she says.

The man tilts his head like this is all entertainment.

"You were supposed to make me rich," he continues. "You took your mother from me. You denied me. You ruined my life."

The room tilts.

I shift closer to Lenni — not touching, just anchoring my presence at her side.

Her mom's voice cracks. "Lennon… what is he talking about?"

Lenni inhales once.

Deep.

Controlled.

This isn't collapse.

This is detonation.

Just truth—spoken like she's been carrying it like a bomb in her chest for years.

"You stuck your hands down my pants when I was thirteen," she says, voice shaking but sharp. "You don't get to ruin anything ever again."

Silence detonates.

Her mom makes a broken sound like something tearing open inside her.

The man's smile falters.

And that's when I understand something critical.

He didn't come here because he thought he'd

win.

He came here because he thought she'd stay quiet.

And she didn't.

I step forward now.

Close enough that he feels me.

"You're done," I tell him quietly.

Not loud.

Not dramatic.

Final.

Then I straighten.

"Call police. Full report. Assault history flagged. Keep him restrained."

Every guard moves.

Lenni doesn't.

She stands there shaking, but upright.

Claiming space.

And I realize something with terrifying clarity:

This wasn't just a breach.

This was a reckoning.

And she just won.

CHAPTER 26
LENNON

Virginia

I thought saying it out loud would shatter me.
It didn't.
It cracked something open, yes. It burned. It shook. It hurt in places I didn't know still remembered.
But it didn't break me.
It set me free.
The morning after feels different.
Not lighter. Not exactly.
Just... clearer.
My mom sits across from me at Hank's kitchen table, fingers wrapped around a coffee mug she hasn't touched. Her eyes are swollen from crying. Mine probably are too.
But there's no panic in the room.
No scrambling.
Just truth, sitting between us like something that finally has a name.
"I should've known," she says quietly.
I shake my head.
"You did know," I tell her. "You just didn't know how deep it went."
Her chin trembles. "I should've protected you."
"You did," I say, reaching across the table and

taking her hand. "You left him."

That was the protection.

She suspected. She felt the shift. She saw the way I stopped sitting near him. The way I flinched when he came into a room.

She didn't have proof.

And I didn't give her any.

Because at thirteen, I thought silence was safer.

Now I know better.

Now I know silence is a cage.

Hank doesn't interrupt.

He stands at the sink, back turned slightly, giving us space without leaving the room. Close enough that I feel him. Far enough that this moment belongs to us.

He hasn't once tried to speak for me.

Hasn't once tried to soften it.

Hasn't once told me to calm down.

He lets me be strong.

That's the difference.

When my mom finally leaves—after a long hug that feels less like goodbye and more like repair—I step outside.

Virginia air hits my lungs, cool and honest.

Hank follows a second later.

He doesn't ask if I'm okay.

He looks at me.

Really looks.

And I see it in his face.

Not pity.

Pride.

"You didn't shake," he says quietly.

"I was shaking," I admit.

"You didn't hide."

That lands somewhere deep.

I step closer.

"I'm done hiding."

His jaw tightens just slightly, emotion held in restraint the way he always does when something matters too much. He lifts his hand and brushes his thumb beneath my eye, catching the faint trace of dried mascara.

Small. Gentle. Certain.

"I know."

The words aren't reassurance.

They're belief.

I glance down at his boots — heavy, worn, planted — and then back up at him.

Without thinking, I slide my bare feet on top of them, rising just enough to close the last inch of space between us.

He doesn't laugh.

Doesn't tease.

His hands come to my waist automatically, steadying but not lifting.

I press a soft kiss to his mouth.

Not hungry.

Not desperate.

Just sure.

And when I pull back, his forehead rests against mine like he's memorizing this version of

me — not the performer, not the survivor.
Just me.

The conference room smells like coffee and fresh printouts.
Not crisis.
Not damage control.
Opportunity.
The new PR manager sits across from me — Merida Collins, sharp blazer, steady eyes, the kind of woman who doesn't flinch when things get messy. She didn't lead with brand strategy when we first spoke.
She led with this:
"What do you want your voice to sound like now?"
Not what plays well.
Not what trends.
What do you want?
That's why she's here.
The rest of the team filters in — my band, my tour manager, my assistant.
No one looks panicked.
No one looks worried.
They look… proud.
Merida clicks her pen once. "Before we get

into scheduling, let's address the elephant in the room."

I brace.

She smiles instead.

"You're trending for the right reasons."

A couple of phones slide across the table toward me.

Fan videos.

Clips of the confession.

Comments scrolling faster than I can read.

She chose herself.

That's our girl.

We've got you.

Protector energy but make it equal.

I swallow.

"We expected backlash," Merida continues. "There was some. But the overwhelming narrative?"

She looks at me directly.

"You took your life back."

Silence settles in the room — but it's not heavy. It's electric.

Ro leans back in her chair. "Merch idea," she mutters. "'Take It Back' tour shirts."

Laughter breaks the tension.

Hank is quiet beside me.

Not looming.

Not hovering.

Present.

Merida folds her hands. "Here's the shift. We're not pivoting away from what happened. We're reframing it. You are not scandal. You are survival. You are strength."

She slides a proposal toward me.

"Long-form interview. Controlled. On your terms. And we lean into the narrative of autonomy. Of boundaries. Of power."

Mila nods slowly. "Fans are celebrating you. They're not clutching pearls."

"They're showing up louder than ever," Merida confirms. "Sales spiked overnight."

I blink.

"Spiked?"

"Twenty percent," she says easily. "You gained more than anyone expected you to lose."

That lands differently than I thought it would.

I don't feel vindicated.

I feel… seen.

Hank's knee brushes mine under the table.

Steady.

Quiet.

Then he clears his throat.

"There's something else," he says.

Every head turns.

He doesn't shift nervously.
Doesn't hedge.

"I opened my own security firm."

The room stills.

Godfrey Security.

The name sits between us.

"We'll be handling all venue sweeps, tour routing, and personal coverage moving forward," he continues. "Independent contract. Direct coordination with management."

Merida raises a brow — impressed, not resistant.

"And that means?" she asks.

"It means," Hank says calmly, glancing at me just long enough for heat to spark behind his restraint, "I'm with her full time."

The air shifts.

Ro grins. "Okay, boss move."

Merida nods once. "I like it. Control stays internal. No external agency politics."

She looks at me.

"You comfortable with that?"

I don't hesitate.

"Yes."

Not because I need him to protect me.

Because I choose him there.

"Then we move forward unified," she says. "Tour messaging stays consistent. No hiding. No shrinking."

No shrinking.

The words echo.

We talk logistics.

Media timing.

Charity partnerships.

Advocacy alignment.

Not survival.

Expansion.

When the meeting wraps, chairs scrape back. Phones buzz. Energy hums like forward motion instead of fallout.

As we walk out of the room, Hank steps ahead of me.

Not pulling.

Not directing.

Just walking.

And then — without turning — his hand drifts behind him.

Two fingers wiggle slightly.

Casual.

Unspoken.

Waiting.

I look down at that familiar, calloused hand reaching back for mine like it's the most natural thing in the world.

Like we've been doing this forever.

I slip my fingers into his.

He doesn't squeeze hard.

Just enough.

Grounded.

Chosen.

We walk down the hallway like that — not hiding, not rushing.

A team aligned behind us.
A future unfolding ahead.

And for the first time in a long time, I don't feel like I survived something.

I feel like I stepped into something.

Bigger.

Stronger.

Mine.

He doesn't look back to check if I'm following.
He knows I am.
Because I'm not being led.
I'm walking beside him.
For the first time in my life, love doesn't feel like something I have to shrink to keep.
It feels like something I can stand tall inside.
And this time—
I'm not surviving the spotlight.
I'm owning it.

NIGHTMARE - HALSEY

THE END

ABOUT THE AUTHOR
C. Marie
is a country-raised storyteller, wife, and mom with a pack of dogs and a couple of chicken coops. She writes romance with feelings, fire, and just enough small-town suspense to keep you turning pages past bedtime.

Off the page, she's concert-goer, a devoted reader, a compulsive note-taker, and a firm believer that iced coffee absolutely counts as a writing tool. She lives where the stars are bright, the roads run narrow, and the characters don't stop talking until the story is told.

BOOKS BY THIS AUTHOR

The Colefield Redemption Series

The Colefield ATV Resort is more than just a getaway — it's the heartbeat of a family bound by grit, loyalty, and love. Passed down through generations whose legacies linger long after they're gone. The resort becomes a refuge for those who've lost their way, a place where second chances take root.

While romance sparks in the most unexpected places, the resort isn't free from turmoil. Violence, loss, and secrets threaten to unravel the peace they've fought for. Yet, through it all, the family stands strong — leaning on each other, protecting their home, and holding fast to the bonds that carry them forward.

Each book in the series follows new and familiar faces as they wrestle with the pull of the past, the promise of love, and the fight to protect not just the resort, but the community and family they've built upon it.

The Linwood Ridge Series

Set in the rugged stretch of Southern Virginia, where the backroads twist through farmland and the mountains rise blue against the horizon, The Linwood Ridge Series follows a tight-knit community bound by loyalty, legacy, and the land beneath their boots. These emotionally charged small-town romances blend heartfelt connection with threads of suspense, exploring the people who fight to hold on to the ridge—and the love that finds them along the way.

Each book in the series stands alone, featuring a different couple whose pasts, secrets, and second chances intertwine with the heartbeat of the ridge itself. Every story is layered with healing, homecoming, found family, and the kind of slow-burn chemistry that makes starting over feel both terrifying and inevitable.

Come home to Linwood Ridge—where love runs deep, pasts run heavy, and every ending is just the start of something new.

Made in the USA
Monee, IL
09 March 2026